Heartless

MICHELLE HEARD

Prologue

DELLA

Life is made up of a series of lies.

Love? It's a fairytale some person made up, so they didn't have to face the cold, hard fact that we are all alone. You come into this world alone, and you leave it alone. Loneliness, it's the one the thing we fear most. It means you're forgotten, you've been rejected, or you're overlooked.

Little girls are told fairy tales of how a prince will come along to sweep them up into their loving arms. From a young age, they are taught that their purpose is to belong. They have to have a family, a husband, children – without this, they are failures.

Little boys are told stories of firemen, policemen, the brave souls who will overcome any evil. They are taught that their purpose is to be the man of the house, to protect, to provide – if they're not able to do this, they aren't men.

They're all lies that most people believe. We create such unnecessary pain for ourselves. You feel like a failure because no- one *loves* you. You only exist if there's someone who sees you. Your life only has worth if you're living for someone else.

That restlessness you feel? It's your soul crying out to be set free from all the deceit you've been forced to believe.

Once in a while, someone will break free from the norm society has created. I want to be one of those people. I want to be *different*. I want to break every damn rule society has ever made for us.

It will mean that I'm alive and not just another sheep wandering aimlessly through life.

Chapter 1

DELLA

"Don't look now, but they just walked in," the redhead whispers excitedly as I start to clear the table.

Rameses, the bar slash diner where I've worked since my first year of college, is always crawling with students.

I place the empty plates on top of each other as her blonde friend looks over her shoulder.

"Fuck, he's so hot. I'd give anything to be screwed by Rhett."

At first, I used to get embarrassed when I heard people talk like that, but after being at college for almost three years, there's very little that shocks me now.

There's not much in the way of dating where I'm from. Hell, I had to go to Polk County High School because Saluda only has an elementary school. Besides the random adventurer traveling through and the summer wave of tourists, the meager population of around seven hundred didn't cater much for dating material.

I glance in the direction of the door and watch as a group of guys walk in. I don't know them that well. I've heard rumors about them, that they're known as the Screw Crew. Every girl wants to be screwed by them, and every guy wants to be one of them. It's really stupid.

They take a seat in my section, and the one with black hair grins at the blonde sitting at the table I'm busy clearing. He bites his bottom lip and winks at her. Damn, even I have to admit that's hot. I might not date, but just like any warm-blooded girl, I appreciate a hot guy when I see one.

The blonde shrieks excitedly and jumps up. "By tomorrow, my name will be on Rhett's screwed list."

The redhead throws some money on the table and follows her friend over to where the guys are. The blonde slides onto the guy's lap, immediately kissing him as if there's no tomorrow. The university should have *making out* as a sport. I swear half the students would qualify for the Olympics.

People don't behave like that back home. Sue, the owner of the Mom 'n Pop diner I used to work at, would be chasing them out the door. After Mom passed Sue took us in. It's because of Sue that I'm able to study for my degree in Graphic Design. Without her generosity, Jamie and I would've been living on the streets. I had been working at her diner for about three months when Mom passed away after her long struggle with cancer. Sue let me borrow money so I could lay Mom to rest. She also took us in. She's old and hard as nails, but she's also the only one who cared about us.

I was ten when Dad died. It was an accident that took him from us. He was out hiking when he tripped over a root and plunged down Big Bradley Falls. After Dad passed, things got bad. Mom was pregnant with Jamie and had to take all kinds of odd jobs to keep the pot going. I was sixteen when Mom passed. Poor Jamie was only six and didn't understand the finality of death. For months she asked where Mom was and when she would come back. Even though we lost our parents early in life, things weren't all bad. Being poor didn't matter as much. I've never been scared of doing an honest day's job. I just want more for Jamie. I want to give her the world, and that won't happen as long as we're stuck in that town. Even though Saluda is only three and a half hours away, it feels like I might as well be from another planet. The people back at Saluda are set in their ways. That's not me. I crave more from life than the monotonous existence that small town has to offer. I want to experience everything life has to offer. I want to be independent. I want to travel. I want to live.

I place the glasses on the tray before taking the dirty dishes back to the kitchen. I studied my backside off to earn this free ride at UNC. The tips I make just about cover the rent. It's not like I need much, anyway. I'm here to study so I can get my degree.

Only six months left and I'll be finished. Then I'll be able to find a good job. I'll go back to Saluda to get Jamie, and we'll leave that town for good. That's my three-step plan. I don't have time for anything else, let alone fooling around. Not that I'm Miss America with a line of guys going around the block, waiting to date her. Hell no, the opposite sex hardly notices me, which is perfectly fine by me. Besides, guys are all horny idiots.

I've heard one of my roommates, Willow, once say, *"Dicks rule, brains drool."*

I share an apartment with three hot girls, like sizzling off the charts hot. Leigh, Willow, and Evie just have to pout, and the guys are all puddles of drool at their feet. They make it easy for me to go by unnoticed, which is a blessing. I might share an apartment with the girls, but we hardly know each other. I'm too busy to hang out with any of them. Come to think of it, sometimes an entire will week will pass by without me seeing Willow or Leigh. Evie is the only one I see every other day.

I walk back out and head over to the table the guys are seated at, noticing that more people have joined them. As I get to the table, I spot Evie. She's glaring at the blonde that's busy devouring one of the guy's faces.

"Are you ready to order?" I ask in general.

Evie tears her eyes away from the couple. When she spots me, a pretty smile pulls at her lips. I wish I had her hair. Because of the natural curl in her ginger hair, she can just wash and go, leaving to air dry. I, on the other hand, have to blow dry my thick brown hair, or it will look like something made a nest in it.

"Hey, sweets. Get me my usual, please," she says. I quickly write down her order of six chicken nuggets. She's addicted to the chicken nuggets we serve here.

"You know her?" One of the guys asks Evie while looking at me. He's got dirty blonde hair with a five-o-clock shadow dusted over a strong jaw. He looks like he could be trouble.

"Yeah, Della's one of my roomies." She points at the two blonde guys she's sitting between and starts to introduce the guys to me. "These two are Jaxson and Marcus." Then she tips her chin at another guy that's busy on his phone. "That's Logan. Jaxson and Logan are twins." She wags her eyebrows playfully. "Double the trouble."

Seeing as they're friends of Evie, I smile at them. It doesn't really matter that she's introducing me to her friends, it's not like I'll remember them tomorrow.

She glares at the black haired guy again. "That's Rhett," she practically spits his name out.

Hell, something must've gone bad between them.

Rhett shoves the blonde from his lap and licks his lips as his dark brown eyes wander over the length of me.

"Why haven't we met you before?" he asks. "I've been at the apartment quite a few times, but I've never seen you there. Trust me, I would remember a face like yours."

I ignore his flirting and answer, "I'm either studying or here at work. I hardly see my roommates."

"I bet you taste sweet," he says, winking at me.

Now I see why Evie doesn't like him. I can't blame her at all. I scowl down at him before looking over the table again.

"Anyone want something from the kitchen? We're closing in twenty."

"I'd take one of you," Rhett tries again.

"You're wasting your time," Evie snaps, irritated.

When he looks at Evie the smile drops from his face. Seconds tick by in silence before he looks back at me. "Are you a carpet muncher?"

"A what?" I frown at him, not in the mood for games. I'm tired, and I still have an assignment I need to finish before I can even think of sleeping.

"Are you into pussies?"

What a jerk.

Probably thinks he's God's gift to women.

I take a deep breath, so I don't give him a piece of my mind. I need this job more than I need the satisfaction of telling him to go to hell.

"I'll have a Dr Pepper, a cheeseburger, and fries," Jaxson suddenly says. It sets off the others, and I quickly write down all the orders. I give Jaxson a grateful smile before taking the order to the kitchen.

When I'm done handing the order over to the kitchen, I head out front to clear more tables. While I'm busy clearing the table next to the one Evie and her friends are seated at, Marcus says, "I bet you a hundred you can't get her to spread her legs."

"I'm a master at getting girls to spread them wide for me. Spreader bars should've been named after me," Rhett jokes, while he pulls the blonde closer to his side. "Isn't that right, babe?"

She nods all dreamily actually falling for his shit.

I shake my head, figuring Rhett already has that hundred in his pocket. The blonde will hump his leg right here if he says the word.

I go get their orders, and as I place Rhett's plate in front of him, he takes hold of my wrist. He tries to pull me closer, but I resist, yanking my hand free from his.

"Come on, babe. You're so damn cold. I'm sure I can find a way to warm you up."

Ignore him, Della. He's just an arrogant jerk.

Ignoring my own warning, I place my hands on the table and lean forward until I'm right in his face. I smile sweetly and bite my bottom lip, just like he did earlier. I watch with satisfaction as his eyes lock on my lips.

"Oh, baby," I groan seductively. A cocky smirk pulls around his lips. He's arrogant enough to actually believe that he stands a chance with me. What an idiot. "You think just because you're hot every girl wants to be with you. The day I let you touch me is the day hell freezes over. There's no way I'm letting your rotten, STD infested dick near me. "

I blow him a kiss and walk away, feeling pleased with myself for putting him in his place.

"Make that two hundred dollars. Like I said, there's no way she's spreading it for you," Marcus says as he starts to laugh.

The words register and I stop dead in my tracks. Slowly, I turn around as my blood starts to boil. I only realize my mistake when a huge smile spreads over Rhett's face. I just fell for their stupid game. The bet is about me.

"Double that," Rhett says as he locks eyes with me. "Four hundred dollars."

Marcus and some of the other guys at the table laugh again. "You're on. Damn, I'm going to enjoy taking your money."

"How stupid are you?" I ask all the guys in general. I seriously doubt they have any kind of brain activity between all of them. "You're making a bet in front of me. Do you really think I'm going to let any of you idiots near me?" I'm angry and offended that they would make a bet about who can screw me first, let alone do it in front of me.

Rhett gets up and walks over to me. I glare at him, wishing I could castrate him with just a look.

He lifts his hand to my face, and I slap it away. "You're seriously a piece of work," I snap, wanting to do him some bodily harm.

"What's going on here?" a deep voice interrupts my thoughts of punching Rhett right in the face.

My eyes dart to the owner of the voice, and for a moment, I forget to scowl. I've seen him with the group a couple of times, but never up close before. Damn, he's hot. The other guys pale in comparison to him. He's much taller than the others, with dark brown hair that's begging to have my fingers tangled in the thick strands. Our eyes lock, and I almost forget to breathe. His eyes are dark pools that would make any girl forget her own name. His jaw's covered with a few days' old stubble, and it only makes him so much more attractive. His shirt's tightly wrapped over a muscled chest. I'd love to find out if it feels as hard as it looks.

Suddenly, Rhett says, "Carter, you're just in time. We have a bet going. Four hundred dollars to whoever gets her to spread them first." The jerk points at me with a thumb. I have a sudden urge to grab it and twist it right off his hand.

For some reason, the stupid bet really bothers me now that Carter is here.

To make things worse, three more guys walk in and come to stand at the table.

"You guys want in?" Marcus adds oil to the fire.

"In on what?" one of them asks.

"Betting pool. Whoever screws her first, wins."

My eyes drift over all the faces around me. Evie mouths 'sorry' to me. Jaxson and Logan are too busy eating to pay attention. Marcus winks at me, and it makes my anger flare back to life.

Before this really gets out of hand, I turn around and walk back into the kitchen. I wait until they leave before I go back out to clear the remainder of my tables. I've worked at Rameses for almost three years. You would think I'd be used to dealing with idiots like the Screw Crew.

The walk home feels much longer tonight. I should've taken my truck. It's old and leaves a massive ball of smoke whenever I pull away, but at least it still runs.

When I get home, the apartment's empty. That's what I like most about sharing with the other girls. When I'm here, I always have the apartment to myself. Sometimes I wonder what it would be like to go out with them, to have close friends I can laugh and chill with. But then I remind myself that I'm not here to make friends. I'm here for Jamie. My sister is all that matters. A month after I finish here, Jamie will be eleven. I need to find a good job and get us a place of our own before she's twelve.

I throw my bag on the single bed. I don't have much in my room, just the second-hand bed and nightstand. I first shower, then make myself some coffee before settling down on my bed. I need to finish the assignment I'm working on even if it takes all night. Luckily it's Sunday tomorrow, and I only have to be at work at twelve, which means I can sleep in.

I get lost in my work until I'm finally happy with it. Grabbing the cup with some cold coffee still left in it, I walk to the kitchen. I'm busy rinsing the cup when I hear the door open. I dry my hands and go to see which of the girls are home. When I see Carter coming in with his arm around Evie, I feel a slight sting of disappointment. I brush the unwelcome feeling away.

"... fucking bitch," he finishes whatever he was busy saying as his eyes land on me.

Damn, those eyes of his have the power to turn my mind to slush.

Then Evie looks up and my lips part with shock when I see her swollen cheek. Mascara is streaked over her cheeks, with red blotches around her eyes. I rush forward and grab Evie away from him.

"Get your hands off her," I hiss.

Was he busy cursing Evie as they came in?

I bring her to the couch and let her sit down. I lift her face up, and with worried eyes, I take in the bruise

17

on her cheek. Her tears make my insides quiver with anger. Evie is one of the kindest people I know. Why would he hurt her?

I turn back to Carter, my body shaking with rage. "Get out!"

He takes a step towards me, and it makes me tense. I'm nothing like my friends. I won't hesitate to introduce my knee to his balls.

"Let me-" he starts to talk, but I cut him off. He can keep his explanation for those air-headed bimbos he likes to screw.

"Nothing you say will make this okay. You're nothing but a spineless piece of shit. Is it a turn-on?" I sneer as I walk towards him. "Does it make you feel like a man?"

"Della," Evie calls from behind me. I need to get back to her. I shove him as hard as I can, and I'm pleased when he takes a step back.

He tilts his head, and there's an expression on his face I can't read. Maybe anger? Who cares anyway? I hate the Screw Crew. They're nothing but a bunch of bullies. I hope they aren't close friends of Evie. She needs to stay away from guys like them. They're nothing but trouble.

I didn't see it earlier, but the brand of shirt he's wearing is of the expensive kind. He reeks of money. That explains it all.

"You should use some of that money and buy yourself some morals," I snap.

To my surprise he laughs, shaking his head at me. His eyes drop to my legs, and it's only then I remember that I'm only wearing a shirt.

Chapter 2

CARTER

White cotton panties. Fuck. She yanks the shirt down and scowls at me.

"Careful, babe. Looking at me like that will get you in trouble," I taunt her just because it's so fucking easy to get her all riled up.

Earlier at the diner, I actually thought she was hot. I admired her for standing up to the guys. I don't have to like her to admit that she's got killer legs, and don't even get me started on her mouth. I'd love to see her on her knees with her lips wrapped around my cock. Then I'll live up to the what she thinks of me as I add her name to the screwed list. She's just another judgemental bitch. I regret standing up for her to my friends, telling them to back off and to drop the bet. I'm going to win that bet just so I can see the look on her face when she realizes that she's nothing but a four hundred dollar fuck.

I watch as her scowl turns to a death glare, but I don't miss the blush creeping over her cheeks. What do you know? Little Miss high and mighty may hate me, but those blushing cheeks are a clear sign that she's attracted to me. That will work perfectly to my advantage.

I grin at her and whisper, "Game on."

She takes another step closer to me, and I get a whiff of her scent. She smells edible, like crushed apples.

There's a slight frown on her forehead when she says, "I have no idea what you're talking about, and I'm not one of your friends." She wiggles a finger between us. "Whatever you think is going on here, it's not. Get out of our apartment before I call the cops. "

"You're quick to judge others, aren't you?" I say as I start to plan all the different ways I'm going to have fun with her. "You're one of those who loves to sit on your high fucking pedestal while passing judgment on anyone who's different from you. Quite fucked up if you ask me."

"I didn't ask you," she snaps, her blue eyes flaming with anger. It makes them look electric.

"No, you didn't," I whisper. "A word of advice, next time make sure of your facts before you jump to conclusions. It will save you from having to crawl back to me with your tail between your legs to apologize. Then again, I'd love to see you on your knees."

I see the moment doubt washes over her face. She's finally second-guessing her actions. That makes me smirk as I lean into her. I watch her eyes widen, and the blush deepens on her cheeks.

"Just remember I didn't start this little game, you did." I lean in more until our cheeks brush, and whisper in her ear, "But I'm sure as hell going to finish it, babe."

She pulls away, her breaths coming fast. "I didn't start anything, and I'm not playing some pathetic game."

She still doesn't understand what she did. "Sweetheart, you were so fucking quick to label me as just some asshole who has too much money and not a lick of decency. Who am I to disappoint you? I'll just have to live up to the image you have of me. I wouldn't want to let a clever little thing like you down."

She glances back at Evie who's been watching us with huge eyes. Before Della can look back at me, I turn around and leave. I'm not going to make it easy for her to apologize. She's going to learn the hard way that I don't let people fuck with me and get away with it.

I'm not sure whether I'm pissed off at her for accusing me being some fucked up rich kid who would hit Evie, or whether I'm turned on by her killer body. I've never felt so confused over a woman before. Why the fuck do I even care what she thinks? It's clear she doesn't think much of me.

I was helping Evie. She and Rhett got into an argument when that psycho blonde that was hanging around Rhett attacked her. I told Rhett to fucking man up and admit that he cares about Evie. I also told him to get rid of the trash. I swear he's fucking everything in sight, so he doesn't have to face the fact that he's fallen for Evie. He keeps denying it but loses his shit whenever another guy just looks at her.

I don't understand why they don't just get together. A blind man can see that they have the hots for each other.

After the psycho blonde slapped Evie, I brought her home to make sure she was okay. I did it because she's a decent person and didn't deserve what happened. I also did it because Rhett is one of my best friends and I know he's going to feel like shit about what happened.

But mostly I did it in the hopes of seeing Della again. Earlier at the diner, there was tension between us and I was curious to find out if it was real. When I'd first walked into the apartment, the tension was there in full force, until she saw Evie's face.

I had every intention of making sure the guys forgot about the damn bet until she got on her judgmental high horse. I've been judged wrongly before, and it never bothered me. Marcus and Rhett are the ones with the screw lists. They're the manwhores responsible for our nickname, Screw Crew. I'm no saint, but I have nothing on those two. As for the twins, Jaxson and Logan, they're not huge on dating. Jaxson keeps busy between college and being a personal trainer, where Logan is the quiet one in the group.

As for me, all my focus is on finishing my degree. Once I've graduated, I'll start working at Indie Ink Publishers. Dad said I have to start at the bottom. I understand why. That's the best way for me to learn everything about the company and the people working there. When I take over from Dad, I want it to be because I deserve it.

On the drive back to the house I share with the guys, my mind goes back to the little spitfire. Even dressed in just a shirt and panties, she handled me like a boss. I have to admire her for standing up for Evie. But fuck, I'll never hurt a woman.

I'm sure as hell going to have some fun with Della.

Chapter 3

DELLA

"You've got it all wrong," Evie says. "Carter only brought me home. He's not the one that hit me. Carter will never hurt me."

Oh shit!

What the hell have I done?

I swing back to the door, and when I see that Carter has already left, an awful feeling settles in the pit of my stomach.

"That blonde bitch slapped me because I got into to a fight with Rhett," she explains. "I really don't understand why he likes those types of girls."

I close the door and walk to the kitchen. I open the fridge and look for something cold. There's not much, so I grab a bottle of water. I wrap a dishcloth around it as I walk back to the living room.

I press it lightly to Evie's cheek. "Just hold it there. It will help with the swelling."

I sit down next to her and sigh. I drop my head back and let out another miserable sigh.

"I accused Carter of hitting you," I whisper. "Dammit, I'm going to have to apologize."

Evie gives my hand a squeeze. "Thank you for looking out for me."

I worry my bottom lip between my teeth. When I make eye contact with Evie, there's only pity.

"Damn, I've screwed up badly, haven't I?"

She nods, dropping the water bottle to her lap.

"Carter's not the kind of guy you insult and get away with it. He's the heartless one in the group."

"Heartless?" I ask. "He made sure you got home safe."

"Only because I have this love-hate thing going with Rhett. Those four guys are Carter's family. He'll do anything for them. I've known him for three years, and he still keeps me at a safe distance."

"So you're telling me not to apologize? I'm not afraid of admitting when I'm wrong."

Evie turns her body towards mine and looks me right in the eye.

"You're only going to waste your time and make things worse. There was this girl who cheated on Jaxson. Carter got her to strip down to her underwear, thinking they were going to have sex. He made her do the walk of shame out of their house in her underwear. Carter doesn't forgive he gets even. It would be better if you just ignore it all. It's not like you see him a lot anyway."

I take the bottle of water from her and open it. I take a few sips, thinking about what she just said. I didn't take him for the cruel kind. Maybe Evie's right? It's not like I see him often. Besides, it's only a few more months before I have my degree. We're from different worlds. Once we leave here, I'll never see Carter again.

Curiosity gets the better of me, and I ask, "Why do you hang out with them? They look like trouble."

She looks deep in thought when she says, "They're not trouble, Della. They're my family. Few people know this, but I had nothing. I was one meal away from starving and living on the street when Rhett found me." She looks around the apartment. "All of this is because of them. They are paying for my studies, for everything I need."

Shock ripples through me. Never in a million years would I have guessed that Evie once lived on the streets.

"What do they want in return?" I ask. No one does anything unless they stand to gain something in return.

She shakes her head. "Nothing. At first, I thought there was a catch. I mean, people just aren't that good, you know? But they have never asked for anything, Della. That's why I love them. They are far from perfect, but they're mine."

I take another sip of water, absorbing everything Evie has told me.

"Who came up with their name, Screw Crew?"

Evie chuckles as she relaxes back against the couch. This is the most we've ever talked. I have to admit I like it a lot.

"That's Marcus. He was the first to start with it. If you've slept with one of the guys, then you're a Screw Crew babe."

"Are you?" I drop my eyes from hers. "Sorry, that's a personal question."

She gives me a sad smile and shakes her head. "No, I'm not. They have this rule that sisters are off limits."

I frown, not following. "But you're not related to any of them."

"They see me as one, so I'm off limits. It's a stupid rule if you ask me. There's only me and Mia, Rhett's sister. Rhett made the rule when Mia turned eighteen. I think Logan is in love with her. If Rhett just looks in my direction then Logan reminds him of the rule. I think he's trying to force Rhett to break it, so he can have a relationship with Mia."

"Logan is the nice one that was on his phone?"

She nods. "He's always on his phone. He thinks no one knows that he's constantly texting with Mia, but I've had a glimpse at the screen."

"Why doesn't Rhett break the rule?"

A sad look shadows Evie's green eyes. "Mia is his world. He'll give up everything to protect her and no one is worthy of dating his little sister."

"She's going to date with or without his permission," I state the obvious. "He can't expect her not to date while he screws everything in sight." There's a flicker of pain on her face, and it makes me regret my words. "Sorry, Evie."

"You're right," she says, shrugging away the pain. "Where Carter is heartless, Rhett is shameless. At first, I used to think that he slept with so many girls to avoid committing to one. With time, I realized that's just a lie I'm telling myself to lessen the pain. He takes care of me and Mia. He's committed to us. I'm just a little sister to him."

"Men are idiots," I grumble.

Chapter 4

CARTER

There's a game on TV, not that I'd be able to tell you who's winning.

I've been sitting here thinking about Della. Normally, I'd think of a suitable punishment to teach her a lesson. The problem is that every scenario I come up with ends with her naked in my bed and screaming my name.

I don't even know her. The two times I've seen her, she looked pretty high maintenance to me. I don't have time for that shit.

I know what people say about me behind my back. I've heard the rumors. I'm heartless. I'm a jerk. Fuck with me and I'll destroy you.

They're not really rumors if they're true.

I don't care a flying fuck about what people think of me. Whether people like me or not doesn't matter at all. Everyone is replaceable in life.

I have my four brothers, Logan, Jaxson, Marcus, and Rhett. I trust them and only them. Evie and Mia are the only females I tolerate. The rest is just a warm place for me to bury my cock.

I have to remember that's all Della is, just another warm body.

Rhett walks into the living room and sits down beside me. A few minutes pass where we just stare at the screen, before he says, "I'm heading to Rameses for something to eat before we go check on Mia."

I give him a look that says I'm not falling for his bullshit act. "Back off from the fucking bet," I growl.

Rhett gets up again and shrugs as he says, "I'm hungry. They serve great food. I've heard the pussy, fuck, I mean the pie is orgasmic."

I get up and grab my keys.

"Where are you going?" Rhett asks as we walk out of the house.

"To grab something to eat," I growl.

He pats me playfully on the back as he starts to laugh. "Yeah, are you in the mood for some pussy, too?"

I stop and stare him down, fighting the urge to punch him. There's a huge smile on his face that makes it hard to stay angry with him.

"Don't fuck with her," I warn. Fuck knows why I'm standing up for the chick. I should hang her out to dry.

Rhett wags his eyebrows. "Then you better win the bet."

Chapter 5

DELLA

When I turn around and see Rhett and Carter taking a seat in my section, I just know that the rest of my day is going to be bad.

For a second I contemplate asking Maggie to help them, but then I suck it up and walk over to them. If I don't face them now, then they'll just keep coming back.

I feel awful for the way I behaved last night. My eyes take in everything about Carter as I weave through the tables, to where they are seated in the corner.

I feel the same twinge of disappointment I felt the night before. This time it's because I treated him unfairly. I'm not that kind of person. I'd like to think that I'm not judgmental, but after my behavior, I need to take a good look at myself.

When I reach the table, Carter doesn't bother to look up from the menu.

"Can I get you something to drink?" I ask.

Rhett grins and leans on the table with his elbows while wagging his eyebrows at me. "I'd like a tall glass of you."

I ignore him and glance at Carter. When he still doesn't look up, I just go for it. "I'm sorry about last night."

He drops the menu to the table, leans back in the chair, and gives me a harsh glare. I start to doodle on my notepad, feeling uncomfortable under his intense stare.

"On second thought," he says as he slides out of the booth. I have to look up to keep eye contact. "I've just lost my appetite."

The look on his face is one of disgust, and it actually hurts knowing it's because of me.

"You're just going to give up on the bet?" Rhett asks. His tone is light and playful, and in total contrast to the tension between Carter and me.

Carter's eyes never leave mine as he takes a step closer to me. I hold my ground, determined to not show him how intimidated I really feel by him. He leans in really close and for one blinding moment I actually think that he's going to kiss me. My heart starts to slam wildly against my ribs, and my stomach is engulfed by a wave of nervous excitement.

Instead of kissing me, he sniffs at me. I suck in a shaky breath as he pulls back.

"Smells like shit to me." His words are cruel and each one stabs at my sense of worth. I can't believe he just said that to me. Now I understand what Evie meant when she said Carter is heartless. He's not just cruel but an asshole as well. I know I shouldn't let him get to me, but damn, it's hard.

I drop my eyes from him and turn back to Rhett. Yeah, I'd rather face Rhett and all his flirting than the hatred I just saw on Carter's face.

"What can I get you, Rhett?" I ask as I fight to keep control of my emotions.

I shouldn't let Carter upset me. Hell, I'm not even sure why his words hurt so much. I've never cared before what people think of me. Besides, it's not like he actually means anything to me.

"Yeah, babe," Rhett says, and this time there's no playful tone. He actually sounds sorry for me. "Let me have a burger and fries."

"And to drink?" I keep my eyes on my notepad as I write the order down, thankful that I have a reason to not look at them.

"Just water."

I walk away, fighting the urge to glance one last time at Carter. I need a moment to catch my breath.

It's been a long day. Everything went wrong. My truck wouldn't start this morning, then there was the thing with Carter. At least, Rhett didn't give me any trouble when I brought his order to him. I even spilled a shake on a customer. Like I said, it's been a long day.

Even though it's past midnight, it's humid which makes the walk home torturously long.

I'm halfway home when I hear music coming from a nearby house. As I get closer to the house where it's coming from, I notice a bunch of cars parked in the driveway and on the pavement. It looks like someone's having a party. It's a wonder no one has complained to the cops, yet.

Most of the houses and apartments in this area are occupied by students.

I'm busy walking by the house when I hear some guy say, "Check it out."

I don't glance back but instead walk a little faster, not sure if they're talking about me or something else.

I become hyper-aware of the footsteps behind me. Dammit, this is the last thing I need.

Someone grabs hold of my arm, swinging me around. My eyes dart over two guys as my breathing speeds up.

"What's the hurry? Come hang with us," the one holding my arm slurs.

Just great! Drunk jerks.

Panic starts to swirl in my chest when I realize how serious my situation is right now. I'm practically alone in the dark with two guys who have clearly had too much to drink.

I try to pull my arm free, not wanting to piss the guy off. When he tightens his hold on my arms, I calmly say, "I'm heading home. Just two houses away. I have people waiting for me." I hope they fall for the lie.

The guy chuckles darkly, then looks at his friend. "You hear that? She has people waiting for her. How stupid do you think we are?"

"The jump from your ego to your IQ would be suicidal," I snap, yanking my arm free.

The guy makes a grab for my arm again, and I just react. I bring my knee up and it connects hard with his groin. The force is enough to make him stagger back with a cry of pain.

I dart around and make a run for it while the one guy is clutching his crushed balls. At least, I hope I crushed them.

"Get the bitch!" The guy yells.

When I hear their footsteps slamming against the road as they come after me, fear explodes in my chest. I push my legs as hard as I possibly can, but their thundering steps keep getting closer.

My chest starts to ache with every breath I take. Panic clamps down on my lungs until all the air is squeezed from them and I can't suck in another breath.

Dark thoughts roll over me in sickening waves.

This is not happening to me.

I swallow back the bile pushing up my throat and try to suck in a painful breath. Digging my nails deeper into my sweaty palms, I focus on every step that brings me closer to home. I need to get away from their perverted clutches.

I can feel them right behind me, and it makes the panic and fear spike sharply in my chest. I'm not going down without a fight. I struggle to get my next breath into my burning lungs, to stay calm for another few precious minutes.

My vision tunnels on the road in front of me.

Keep your shit together, Della. Almost, babe, you're almost there.

You can make it.

I want to sag down to the floor and just curl into a ball. My lungs are burning something fierce. But I can't stop running because that will mean that I'm giving up, and I'm not a quitter.

Suddenly, a car swerves in front of me, coming to a screeching halt half over the pavement.

My stomach sinks heavily as it blocks my way. When I swerve to run around the back of it, one of the guys catches up to me. His fingers dig into my arm, yanking my body back.

As I lose my balance and slam against the guy, I want to scream for help, but there's nothing but my terrified breaths escaping my lips.

I fight to get my balance back and wrench my arm free from his grip. As I turn to run, I slam hard into something. Arms come around me, and I finally find my voice. I let out a frightened shriek, hoping the occupants of one of the nearby houses will come to my rescue.

The person takes hold of my chin, but I rip my face away. "Let go of me!"

His arm tightens around me, and this time when he takes hold of my chin, there's no pulling away. He nudges my face up until our eyes meet. The second I see that it's Carter my blood runs cold.

Is all of this because of the fight last night? No one can possibly be that cruel?

"Are you okay?" he asks, but the words don't register through all the fear. I push against his chest, trying to get free.

"Della," he snaps, and I instantly freeze. "Fuck," he hisses, then I'm shoved into another pair of arms. "Hold her while I deal with these fuckers."

My eyes are wide and watering. When I look up at Rhett, I almost start to cry.

"Let me take her," a gentler voice says. My head snaps toward it and when I see that it's Logan, I actually feel a flicker of relief. Logan doesn't look like the kind of man who will hurt someone, especially not a woman.

He pulls me away from Rhett, and I willingly go, hoping I'm not wrong about him.

"Come on, man." One of the guys that were chasing me whines. "We saw her first."

When I hear the same guy grunt, I glance over my shoulder. Carter, Marcus, Rhett and Jaxson circle the two guys. I see the moment the guys realize that they're in trouble.

Carter throws a punch, slamming his fist against the jaw of the guy that grabbed me.

Only then do I start to understand what's happening. The guys stopped to help me.

Logan turns me away from the group as they start to beat the two assholes.

"You don't want to see this. Get in the car," Logan says.

"They're not your friends?" I ask, needing to make sure that I'm not in trouble anymore.

"We don't associate with trash," Logan grinds out as he opens the backdoor.

I slide inside with Logan following behind me. When he pulls me into his arms, I curl up against him, glad to finally be safe. My heart is still beating wildly and I feel dizzy from the fright.

I focus on my breathing as the sounds of grunts and punches fill the night.

When the other men get back into the car, things get really awkward. There's not enough space in the back for four of us. Rhett slips in on my right side. When he pulls me onto his lap, I almost start to fight. But then I see his bloody knuckles, and I let him hold me. He won't hurt me after fighting for me. At least I hope he won't.

"You okay, babe?" His voice is like a cold shower on my overheating brain.

I drop my chin to my chest so they won't be able to see the lingering fear and embarrassment on my face.

Rhett surprises me by placing a kiss to my hair as he pulls me against his chest. His arms circle me protectively and he holds me tightly.

44

He just holds me. There are no perverted remarks. No flirting.

Gosh, I need this so much. It's like a soothing balm on my frail nerves.

When they park in front of my apartment block, I hear Carter ask, "Why the fuck were you walking the streets in the middle of the night?"

Logan gets out first. I start to move, but Rhett slides out of the car, taking me with him. He keeps an arm around me for which I'm thankful. Maybe he'll keep Carter from killing me.

I glance up, but when I see the anger on Carter's face, I quickly look away.

Wrapping my arms around my waist, I whisper, "My truck wouldn't start this morning."

"So you decide to go for a fucking midnight stroll and endanger yourself?" he grinds the words out.

The shock of the night starts to wear off, and I scowl at Carter.

"I can't fucking fly, asshole!"

Anger rips through me, and I yank away from Rhett. I start to walk away, but my anger gets the better of me.

"What is it to you anyway?" I say, my voice dangerously close to sounding hysterical.

He stalks towards me, his long legs making quick work of the short distance between us.

The sudden close proximity of his body makes my pulse rate spike. Confusion swirls in my mind and I feel like a bug, ass-splatting against a windshield.

Rhett again surprises me when he steps in front of me, shielding me from Carter with his body.

"You need to calm down. She's had a hell of a night. I'm taking her up."

Rhett takes hold of my hand and pulls me away from Carter. I feel like a zombie as I trail behind him.

When we get to my apartment, he holds out his hand to me. "Give me the key, babe."

I start to dig in my bag, and when I find them, I hand it over with a trembling hand.

A headache is starting to pulse right behind my eyes.

Rhett opens the door and lets me walk in first. It's quiet in the apartment. I'm not sure if the other girls are home.

I walk into the kitchen and get myself a bottle of water and some aspirin. Only when I've swallowed it down, do I see that the guys have all come inside.

"What's wrong with your truck?" Jaxson suddenly asks, catching me a little off guard with his question.

I clear my throat and take a breath before answering him. "It just makes this whining sound when I turn the key."

"Give me the keys and I'll take a look at it for you."

I force a smile to my numb face as I take the key from my keychain. When I hand it to Jaxson, I whisper, "Thank you."

"Are you going to be okay?" Logan asks.

Damn, the twins are turning out to be amazing guys. Even Rhett, if I have to be honest with myself. Marcus hasn't said anything yet. I'm thankful for that. The last thing I have strength for is some wiseass comment about the stupid bet.

"I'm fine," I say, trying to force one last smile to my face. I just need a shower and sleep.

I watch Marcus, Logan, and Jaxson leave. Rhett places his arm around my shoulders and gives me a sideways hug. "Try to get some rest, babe."

I nod, suddenly feeling the sting of tears behind my eyes. I never expected Rhett to be so nice. It seems I've been wrong about them all. They must think I'm such a bitch.

When Rhett notices that Carter isn't leaving, he stops.

"I'll be fine," I whisper, not wanting to prolong this night any longer than I have to.

Carter watches until Rhett is out of the apartment before he turns back to me.

"Why were you out so late?" he asks again.

I pinch the bridge of my nose. "I was coming back from work."

"You couldn't get a ride with someone?"

I shake my head, not ready to explain that I don't have *a someone* to ask favors of.

"Give me your phone," he whispers, the bite now gone from his voice.

I give him a cautious look, not trusting the peace for one second.

"Just give me your fucking phone," he bites out.

I scowl at him as I pull my mobile from my bag. Reluctantly, I hand it over.

I watch him punch in his number as he growls, "You're fucking stubborn."

He hands the phone back to me. "Don't ever walk at night again. Phone me and I'll come get you."

My scowl turns to a what-the-hell look. Did I bump my head and now I'm hallucinating? Maybe it's the shock that's making me see and hear things?

"Don't give me that look," he says as he starts to walk towards the door. "Lock it behind me and get your ass in bed."

I do what he says, locking the door behind him. Then I just stare at it, trying to figure out what the hell happened tonight.

Chapter 6

CARTER

Fuck, that woman has a death wish.

What angers me most is that it happened down the street from our house. If we weren't driving back from visiting with Mia, we wouldn't have been there to help her.

A chill ripples down my spine at the thought of what could've happened. Della is Evie's roommate. That's the only reason I'm upset, because I know how upset Evie will be.

I'm going to make sure those two fuckers get kicked out of UNC. No woman is safe as long as they're around.

We're all quiet on the way home. Once I've parked the car, we head inside. I go straight to my room. Before I can close the door behind me, Jaxson says, "I'll fix her truck tomorrow."

I want to bite out that I don't care if they set the fucking truck on fire, but the fact that it's a lie keeps the words from spilling over my lips.

"Thanks," I whisper instead.

I shut my bedroom door and yank my shirt over my head. I'm just about to head to the shower when Rhett comes in.

"It's late," I snap.

"It's late," the fucker mimics me, pulling his face like a damn toddler. He falls on my bed. "Why are you such a bastard to her?"

I glare at him, but I should know by now that it won't intimidate Rhett.

"You're like a turd that won't come out. Fucking annoying man," I snap at him.

He sits up, a serious look on his face, which is rare.

"And you're so fucking stuck up, dude. Do you have a ruler rammed up your ass? Cause I'll pull it out and beat you with it."

"You and what fucking army," I say, knowing we're both just pissing in the wind. We'll never get violent with each other.

Rhett gets up from the bed and comes to stand in front of me. "All jokes aside, you need to ease up on her."

"I wouldn't want to disappoint little miss high and mighty."

"What are you talking about?" He frowns at me.

"When I took Evie home, Della assumed that it was who had hit Evie."

"Oh," he says, rubbing his hand over his day old beard. "Is that why she apologized earlier?"

"Yeah."

"And you're not going to let it go?"

"No."

"Why?" he asks.

"Why fucking not?" I snap back.

"Look," Rhett says as he starts to walk towards the door. "I get that you have to follow in your old man's footsteps but that doesn't mean you have to be a dick like him. "

Rhett closes the door behind him.

Only when I'm in the shower do I think about what he said. All my life Dad has lectured me on how I should behave. It got really bad after his first heart attack. It's as if he switched over to panic mode, scared he won't be around to make sure I become the man he wants me to be.

I know he loves me. He only wants the best for me. My mother split before I was out of diapers. My old man raised me while running a billion-dollar empire. He could've passed me off on a nanny, but he didn't. Until I was old enough to stay at home alone, I was either at school or at the office with him.

He worked his ass off to make sure I would always be taken care of. Fuck, he even paid for this house so we could all live together. He's paying for all of our studies, giving me three years of being with the guys before I have to join Dad in New York. He didn't have to do that. He could've stuck me in a college near him. Hell, he could've forced me to start working right out of school. I owe him a lot. I can't let him down.

I know Rhett is right. I'm becoming just like my father.

I'll ease up on Della but I'm sure as hell not going to kiss her ass.

Chapter 7

DELLA

Dammit, I was going to be late. I only had one class on Mondays, but it might as well have been a life sentence with the amount of sleep I got last night.

I rush down the stairs but come to a sudden halt when I see the guys working on my truck.

I tilt my head, frowning. This is the last thing I expected to see. I walk a little closer, not sure how to handle them after everything that happened.

"Morning," I say to get their attention.

I get a rumble of 'mornings' in return but only Rhett and Carter stop working.

Rhett gives me a hug before his eyes travel over me. This time it's not a perverted look, but one of concern.

"How do you feel, babe?"

I can't help but smile at him. I get a feeling that Rhett has the softest heart buried beneath his manwhore image he's trying to blind everyone with.

"I'm good." I glance at my watch. "I'm going to be dead if I don't get to class now."

I start to turn away when Carter says, "We're taking you."

Stunned, I can only stare at his back as he walks to his car. It's not the same SUV from the night before. This morning he's driving an old mustang that looks vintage and expensive.

I glance at Rhett, wanting to make sure whether Carter is serious about taking me to class. Rhett just shrugs but at least he's coming with, so I won't be alone with Carter.

I don't know what to make of Carter. He's one hell of an enigma that I'll never figure out. It sucks that I like him so much. I would even go as far as to admit that I have a crush on him. Not that I'm happy about it. I never thought I'd fall for someone like Carter. I don't usually go for the strong badass type. Logan is more my type, the strong silent kind.

Carter? Hot as sin on the outside but cold as ice on the inside.

Yeah, who would've thought a day would come where I'd willingly subject myself to Rhett's company. I'm just thankful I can use him as a buffer between me and Mr. Heartless.

The ride to campus is awkward. When I glance to the front, Carter's eyes catch mine in the review mirror, so I've resorted to staring out the window.

"You should come this weekend," Rhett suddenly says, breaking the thick tension in the car.

Carter scowls at him, and that only makes me curious.

"To what?" I ask even though I have plans to go back home. I visit Jamie every second weekend when I have time off from work.

"We're having a party."

I'm definitely not in the mood for a party with the Screw Crew. From what I know from them, there will be naked women everywhere.

"I have plans."

"Can't you take one night off from work?" Rhett asks.

"Oh, I'm not working this weekend." Carter's sharp gaze locks on mine and for some reason I feel like I have to explain. "I'm going home to see my sister."

"You're full of shit, Della. Everyone's going to be at the party. It's Friday night. You can still go visit your sister. You can also tell Evie to get her ass over there or I'm going to have to drag her there myself. You might as well come along. You chicks like to travel in packs and hold hands."

Rhett's right. I'll only be leaving early Saturday morning anyway.

I can't help but smile. "What makes you think Evie will listen to me? Besides, you've know her longer. Ask her yourself."

Rhett glances at me from between the seats, widening his eyes. "Hell no, I'm in the dog house. She'll rip my balls off if I talk to her now."

"And you want me to ask her to a party where you'll be?" I'm really starting to like Rhett.

"Yeah, you don't have balls to lose. Besides, she'll be all calmed down by the weekend."

"Fine, only because I owe you one for last night. I'll ask Evie, but I'm not guaranteeing anything, and I can't stay too late."

The campus is crazy busy and Carter has to double park.

58

"Rhett, drive around the parking area. I'll be back in a few minutes," Carter says as he gets out.

"Have a good day, Rhett," I say as I slip out.

As I walk around the front of the car, Rhett yells, "When does the class finish?"

"In two hours," I say as I start to cross the road.

"Watch out," Carter snaps.

His strong fingers clamp around my arm and he yanks me back. I lose my balance from the sudden jerk, and my body slams into his. My hands land on his chest and it doesn't escape me that it feels as hard as it looks.

"Are you fucking suicidal?" he growls.

My eyes snap up to meet his. They are dark and hard. The grim line around his mouth only makes him look more gorgeous. I'm starting to hate that I find him so attractive. It's really confusing liking someone you don't like.

"Why do you have to be such a jerk?" I pull away from him but this time I look left and right before crossing the road.

I pick up my pace but then Carter starts to walk beside me. I glance up at him, wondering where he's heading.

59

"Do you have a class?" I haven't seen him on this side of the campus before.

"No, I'm making sure you don't break your pretty little neck before you get to class," he says, sounding irritated.

What a jerk!

Offended, I stop and glare daggers at him. "I don't need a babysitter."

"You sure?" he says as he comes to stand in front of me. "It sure as hell looks like you need one."

My eyes dance over the strong features of his face. He has a killer smoldering look and kissable lips.

No, Della! Focus. You can't drool over his looks while you need to be angry.

"Pity you're a heartless dick." Only once the words are out between us, do I realize that I said them out loud.

Ugh.

With one step he closes the distance between us, his chest pressing against mine.

Oh wow. This is an overload for my hormones.

I notice some of the students are stopping to watch this little interaction between us. It doesn't even look like Carter is noticing any of them.

I'm surrounded by his smell, his masculine woodsy scent, something natural, not spicy like most of the other guys drown themselves in.

I can feel his hard muscles pressing against my softness, every unyielding inch of Carter. Heat swirls in my stomach and pushes all the way up to my neck.

"Della," he whispers. It sounds like a warning.

Shit. No. Don't talk to me now, not while I'm drooling over you.

Dammit, he's going to see how overwhelmingly aware I am of him. My plan to fly under the radar can't backfire now. I've been doing such a good job of hiding my insane feelings for him the past two days.

I clear my throat and suck in a deep breath, hoping to cool myself down before he can feel the heat waves coming from my body. All I get is another lung full of Carter.

Lifting his hand, his fingers wrap around the back of my neck. The touch is electric, almost short-circuiting my brain. His thumb skims the heated skin under my ear, sending a lightening streak straight to the spot between my legs.

That's me, I'm done for. No use in trying to hide anything anymore.

He tips my head back and I have no choice but to look into his penetrating eyes. As our eyes meet and lock, a jolt shoots through my stomach.

I'm so screwed right now.

Chapter 8

CARTER

Looking down at her, I can honestly say that she aggravates the living hell out of me.

It's not that I'm scared of a challenge. I mean, damn, I'm going to be working my ass off for the next three years, before Dad retires. It's definitely not the challenge I'm afraid of.

She's too beautiful, the breathtaking, heartbreaking kind. I'm becoming obsessed with this girl and I don't like it at all.

This is fucking bullshit. She has an irritating habit of pressing all my wrong buttons. She's constantly saying something to piss me off. I should hate her, but all I want to do is hold her.

Her skin is silky soft beneath my fingers. Her eyes are wide and totally focused on me. She looks at me in a way no one has ever looked at me.

To most, I'm a walking bank. To Dad, I'm the future of his company. To the guys, I'm a brother. To women, I'm a walking cock.

What am I to Della?

Her tongue darts out, wetting her bottom lip. My heart spasms as her lips part and a blush creeps over her cheeks.

"Carter?" she whispers, as an uncertain look dawns over her face.

She confuses the ever-loving fuck out of me but hearing her breathe my name does something to me. It makes me lose control of the firm grip I have on my life.

My mouth crashes against hers. Her hands shoot up and she grabs hold of my biceps. She pulls slightly away, a look of shock on her face while her lips part again on a shocked breath.

I tighten my hold around her neck and crush her mouth underneath mine. I bring my other arm around her and fanning my fingers over her lower back, I press her against me.

She feels so good against me. I want to hear her scream my name. Damn, I want to be buried deep inside this woman.

And I fucking hate that she's making me feel all these unwanted emotions.

It only makes me kiss her harder. I plunge my tongue inside her mouth and our tongues continue to fight this war between us.

Her hands slip up and over my shoulders. She sucks in a breath as her fingers trail over my jaw.

Somewhere a car backfires, yanking me back to the present.

I pull away from Della, my eyes burning over her face. The blue of her eyes looks like midnight. Her lips are wet and swollen, and the whole look makes her fucking stunning.

She brings a trembling hand to her mouth and her eyes dart around us. It's only then I notice the students watching us.

There's a sinking feeling inside of me. I wasn't supposed to kiss her.

I don't even fucking like her.

I glare down at her. "Taste like shit," I spit the words out.

Shock washes over her features as her eyes well up with unshed tears.

I walk away from her, not waiting to see what damage my words are causing. The more she hates me, the better. I don't need her sniffing around me.

I'm Carter Hayes. I'm fucking heartless. I don't care about the beautiful blue-eyed girl behind me. I don't want her. She means nothing to me. Besides, all I know of women is that they're quick to run, just like my mother did. None of them ever stick around.

I'm almost done with my MBA degree, then I'll take over as CEO of the largest publishing house in the New York. I can't let Dad down. He's sacrificed so much for me, letting me study away from home so I could be with my friends. The last heart attack almost took him from me. It's time for him to retire. I don't want him dying in that office.

Chapter 9

DELLA

My life has returned to normal, which means things have been pretty uneventful. Since the guys fixed my truck, I've only seen Rhett a couple of times when he'd come into the diner. I didn't go to the party and luckily no one asked why. I haven't seen Carter since the kiss which has also been a bonus.

I know he did it only for show, but my mind keeps playing tricks on me. The kiss felt so real. Honestly, I've never been kissed like that.

But the thought of the kiss turns sour when I remember his words.

I smell like shit. I taste like shit.

He's made it pretty clear what he thinks of me. Not like it really matters. For a stupid second, I lost sight of my goals. Never again.

Went I went to visit Jamie, Sue didn't look well. She kept coughing horribly. She blamed it on the flu, but I could see the worry in Jamie's eyes. When I asked Jamie how long Sue had been sick for, she said weeks. It feels like I'm running out of time. If something happens to Sue, I don't know what I'll do. I can't bring Jamie here, which means I'll have to move back to Saluda and commute back here for my exams. The gas money alone will eat up most of my savings.

I need to focus all my energy on my studies. Exams are starting next week. I just have to get through the next few weeks. Everything will be okay. It just has to be.

I ready all the study materials for my first exam, then quickly run to the kitchen. I grab two bottles of water and an apple. On the way back to my room, the front door opens. Willow, Leigh, and Evie all laugh as they come in. The three of them have been spending a lot of time together. Evie tried to include me, but I had to decline. Between working extra hours and studying my ass off, I hardly have time to eat.

When the guys follow the girls inside, I rush into my room and kick my door closed.

I place the bottles and apple at the foot of my bed, then sit down in front of my books and laptop, crossing my legs.

I do my best to block out the voices and laughter, and to focus on the words in front of me.

A knock on my door, makes me sigh miserably. I don't have time for any of them.

"Della," Rhett calls from the other side of the door. My shoulders slump in defeat. I really wanted to get a full night of studying in.

There's a series of knocks, each followed by, "Della." *Knock.* "Della." *Knock.* "Let me in, Della. You know you want to. You can only resist my charm for so long. Give in, babe. Admit you're dying to see me."

I start to laugh at his silliness. Crawling off the bed, I go to open the door. Rhett has a huge smile plastered all over his face.

He wags his eyebrows at me. "Love the shorts and socks, babe. The look totally suits you."

I glance down at my clothes. I'm wearing a white, long-sleeve shirt, pink striped shorts, and socks that reach to my knees.

"It's comfy," I retort.

"How are you doing, babe?" There's a sincere look in his eyes, which draws a smile to my face.

"I'm good. I just have a lot of studying to do. Exams start next week."

He leans in, giving me a hug. It feels so good to be held by someone that I close my eyes to absorb the moment. Sometimes I forget how much I miss touching another human.

I'm just about to shut the door behind Rhett, when Carter slams his hand against it. The warm feeling I have from talking with Rhett turns icy when my eyes meet Carter's.

I try to shove the door closed, but he only moves closer and blocks me with his body. In a hurry to get away from him, I let go of the door and walk over to my bed. I sit down in front of my books and force my eyes to focus on the words.

I hear the door close, but before I can let out a sigh of relief, I hear him move.

Shit!

I steel myself for the fight and glare up at him. "You can leave the same way you entered."

A smile tugs at his lips, drawing my attention to them. It makes me remember what it felt like to have his mouth on mine. Hell, heaven has nothing on that kiss. It was pure euphoria. His kiss had the power to wipe out everything around me, my past, my problems, my uncertain future, and even my dreams. It transported me to a world I didn't even know existed.

Of course, it turned to *shit* the second he opened his mouth.

Suddenly, he says, "You look like shit."

My mouth actually drops open. I shouldn't be surprised or hurt. But I can't help feel the stab of rejection, the pain of being overlooked as a human being. When someone treats you so harshly, you can't help but feel like a waste of space.

I swallow the hurt down and grind my teeth as I hiss, "Like your opinion actually matters. Don't let the door hit you on the way out."

Instead of doing as I asked, he picks up the apple and looks at it with disgust. "This isn't food," he snaps.

I frown, thrown by the sudden change of topic.

"You're a skinny fucking shit, Della. You need to eat more."

Again, my mouth drops open and I can only stare at him in shock and anger. Unlike him, I can't afford to eat three square meals a day. I have to save every cent for Jamie.

To my horror, I watch as he pulls his wallet from his back pocket. He takes out a couple of notes and tosses it on the bed.

I start to shake my head, not being able to process what's busy happening.

Rage washes over me and I dart from the bed. I scoop up the money and shove it hard against his chest.

When he makes no move to take it from me, another wave of rage washes over me wiping out every bit of my self-control.

I grab hold of his belt and shove the money down his pants. That's the closest my hand has ever been to that part of the male body. I'll die of embarrassment later. Right now I'm seething.

I shove him away from me and walk back to my bed. My body is shaking with anger as I sit down.

"You're a self-absorbed jerk," I snap. Once I'm angry, it takes me forever to calm down. I also don't think clearly. I lean back against the wall and bring my knees up. Glaring at the asshole, I open my legs wide.

"Is this what you want? For me to spread my legs. Should I look all achy and needy for you?" His eyes drift over my body and it's hard to miss how they darken. "It will never happen, Carter. Contrary to popular belief, not everyone wants to be on your screwed list."

He moves so fast, pouncing on me before I can even take a breath.

His hard body presses me into the mattress as his mouth slams into mine. I grab at his hair with the full intention of yanking him away from me, but then his tongue shoves past my lips, driving its way forcefully inside my mouth.

His one arm pushes in behind me and he lifts me from the bed, crushing my body to his. He pulls me down and drops his full weight on top of me. Feeling all of him on top of me is incredible.

I feel his hard bulge right between my legs. His teeth and tongue make quick work of any resistance I wanted to put up. My mind clouds over as an aching feeling starts to pulse between my legs.

I've never felt like this before. I hate him but I want him. I want to push him away but at the same time, I want him to strip me bare. I hate myself for wanting him.

Chapter 10

CARTER

Feeling her lips trembling against mine, her soft body melting into me, and the heat radiating from her pussy, makes me lose my mind.

I want to fuck her out of my system. Since that fucking kiss the other day, I can't stop thinking about her. She's poison, slowly spreading through me until there's more of her than there is of me.

Her hands travel to my shoulders and she starts to push against me. I pull her body further beneath mine, but then she breaks the kiss. She gasps for air as she shoves hard at my shoulders. Stunned, I sit back and watch as she almost falls off the bed in her hurry to get away from me.

"You can't do that," she whispers as tears start to spiral over her cheeks. Her flushed face quickly pales and she wraps her arms around her waist.

I have that same sinking feeling I had after our first kiss.

"You can't just come into my room and practically assault me."

For a moment I actually feel bad, but then she goes and accuses me of shit once again.

Anger flares up, and I take a step towards her.

"Rhett!" she screams. She runs for the door, darting right by me. "Rhett!"

The door slams open and she collides with the side of it. I wince knowing it has to hurt. I might not like her but I really don't want to hurt her. I just wanted to teach her a lesson.

Rhett catches her arm and his worried eyes go from her tear-streaked face to me. He pulls her into his arms and it only makes her cry harder.

"Make him leave," she sobs.

Anger tightens his features as he makes eye contact with me. He shakes his head and ushers Della out of the room. When I get to the door, all the guys are on their feet.

"What the fuck did you do?" Jaxson asks as he walks towards me.

"I just kissed her," I spit out. I don't need this shit. "She's fucking crazy."

I stalk out of the apartment, not in the mood for drama.

When I get home, I've cooled down a little. Enough to know that I was a fucking asshole to Della. That is twice now that I've kissed her without her permission.

Even though she kissed me back, it doesn't change the fact that I basically forced myself on her.

The front door slams open and Rhett stalks towards me. When he throws a punch, I do nothing to stop him. I deserve it.

His fist connects with my left cheek and my head whips back from the force. Pain shudders through me, but I keep standing, looking him dead in the eye.

"She's a fucking woman," he shouts. "You never use your strength against a woman. You're not fucking stronger to hold them down. You're stronger to protect them, asshole."

I nod, knowing he's right.

"Don't you fucking do that. You don't get off so easily," he hisses.

He shakes his head and it fucking sucks to see the disappointment on his face.

"I didn't mean to hurt her," I say.

"What did she do to you that you hate her so much?" He throws his arms wide.

At first, I don't plan on answering him, but then the words rush from me. "She's under my fucking skin. I won't let her do to me what my mother did to my dad."

Rhett frowns at me. He takes a step closer to me until we're eye to eye. "That's fucked up. She's not your fucking mother, dude. She's an innocent woman."

"I know she's not my fucking mother," I shout back. "Believe me, I fucking know."

"Oh man," Rhett says as understanding dawns on his face.

I'm glad one of us understands this fucking mess, cause I sure as hell don't.

"What?"

"You're not fighting her," he says, sounding surprised. "You're fighting yourself for liking her."

"I don't like her," I growl.

Deep down I know I'm talking shit. I do like her and it's scaring the shit out of me.

"You don't kiss women you don't like." Rhett starts to leave but at the door, he looks back at me from over his shoulder. "The really fucked up part is that she blames herself. She says she enticed you. That she pushed you too hard. You need to make things right with her."

I just stare at him as he leaves, because he's right. I owe Della an apology.

It feels like I'm losing my mind and it's all because of her.

I don't like her because I like her. How fucked up is that?

Chapter 11

DELLA

Between my studies and working every extra hour I can squeeze in, I'm dead on my feet as I grab my bag.

It started raining an hour ago. I didn't come with my truck because I'm trying to save on gas money.

When I step out of the dinner, it's pouring buckets. At least it's warm. I start to walk up the street and within minutes my shirt and shorts are wet. My sandals start to squeak with every step I take, so I stop and take them off.

Bright lights fall over me as a car pulls up to the curb. The window rolls down and Carter leans over the passenger seat. "Get in."

I give him my most dignified glare, considering that I look like a soaked cat.

He closes the window, but instead of driving away, he switches off the car and gets out.

I sigh loudly, really not in the mood for another fight with him.

He comes to stand in front of me and I'm surprised when the usual scowl he always has around me, is nowhere in sight.

"Look, I'm sorry for being a dick to you."

His apology catches me off guard. I blink up at him through the raindrops, not sure if I can trust this sudden act of peace.

When I apologized to him, he told me I smelled like shit. I should return the favor.

"Oh." The word falls lamely from my tongue, instead of me telling him to go to hell.

I don't know what else to say. I rock back on my feet. He keeps looking down at me as the air tenses between us. I swear, I'm a sucker for punishment when it comes to this guy.

I pull my wet shirt away from my chest and swallow hard. I better just accept his apology and make a run for it before he changes his mind. This kind of *shit* just isn't for me. This is no way to keep a low profile.

"It's fine." I try to think of something else to say, but again I come up empty-handed. *Screw this.*

I turn to leave but disappointment starts to swirl inside of me. I'm hurt that Carter thinks an apology can atone for everything he's done.

I turn back and I'm slammed with the full force of Carter's penetrating dark eyes.

Spit it out, and haul ass girl.

"I tried to make things right after I judged you unfairly, but you wouldn't accept my apology. You told me I smell like shit, Carter. Who says something like that to a person? I'm not dismissing what I said to you, but at least I was standing up for my roommate. You just attacked me because you got some sort of perverted pleasure from hurting me."

"I'm sorry, Della," he says again. There's still no trace of disgust on his face.

"Why?"

Droplets of water trail over his face and I can honestly say I've never seen anything more beautiful in my life. The most beautiful things in life always come at a high price. I'm not sure I can afford whatever price I have to pay to have Carter in my life.

"I'm fucked up."

I shake my head at his lame excuse. I somehow expected more from him.

"We're all fucked up, Carter. You don't see the rest of us being total assholes about it."

Again he nods. I really don't like this side of him. It leaves me feeling frustrated.

I turn around and start to walk away, done with this very weird conversation.

"You smell like crushed apples," he says, and the words stop me dead in my tracks. "You taste like crushed apples," he whispers as he moves closer to me.

I turn back to him. "Then why did you say those things to me?"

"Because I can't stop thinking about crushed apples. I've become obsessed with the smell of it. I can't get enough of the taste of it."

Not sure I'm following him, I ask, "What are you saying?"

"I don't deserve the chance but I'd like one," he whispers as he takes another step closer to me.

"A chance?" I shrug, wishing he would just spit it out.

"With you," I can barely hear the words above the rain.

I close my eyes, shaking my head.

When I open my eyes, he reaches for me. He pulls me to his chest and hugs me, as if we're actually friends.

"Why do you kiss and hug me?" I try to squirm away but he won't let me. "I don't understand why you're even here," I huff upset, but my voice loses its force, going from intense to soft, as my bravery fizzles out.

The longer I keep looking up at him, the more I want to stand in his arms and forget why I was pushing him away in the first place. I want to forget that we've been fighting and all the cruel things he's said to me.

I drop my gaze to his chest and I'm just about to pull away when he says, "I like you, Della. At first, I fought my feelings for you. That night you were running from those guys, seeing the fear on your face, it fucking slayed me. After that, I thought if I could make you hate me, I wouldn't have to fight my attraction for you."

His hands move from my back up to my shoulders. One keeps going until his fingers wrap around the back of my neck. He doesn't wait for me to answer, he just keeps going. My mouth drops open because here is Carter of all people telling me what, exactly?

"I like you way too much to just let you go," he chuckles and it makes him only sexier.

"Just a heads up," I say. "You're not a kid anymore. Pulling my hair won't get me to like you."

"So you're not into kinky shit?"

I scowl at him. "You know what I mean."

He pulls me closer until my chest is flattened against his. I can feel his heart racing as fast as mine. His eyes are smoldering, almost black. I've never seen them so dark. I've always considered myself a strong person, but when I'm around Carter all my so-called strength vanishes into thin air. Love just makes you an idiot.

When he continues, his voice is softer. "I'm a heartless jerk. I'll understand if I've fucked any chances of us getting together."

His fingers slide a hot path down my left arm, takes hold of my hand and he brings it up between us, placing it on his chest. I watch how his hand swallows mine whole.

Carter likes me? I mean, does he really, really like me? Like the way I like him?

Not that I should like him at all. I'm not just going to forget how cruel he's been, no matter how good a kisser he is, or how I feel about him.

"Why are you a heartless jerk?"

He just shakes his head, so I don't force the subject.

I let my eyes drink in every inch of Carter's strong features. No one does it for me like he does. I want a chance with him, but I'm not convinced that I can trust him. I want to fall hopelessly in love but what if this is all just a way of getting me to let my guard down?

I lift myself up on my toes and with a thundering heart, I pray I'm not making a total ass of myself. I let my hands slip up to Carter's neck, but I can't bring myself to go higher than his jaw.

The tingles in my abdomen are going to explode into full-blown fireworks any second now.

I exhale slowly when my mouth reaches his ear. *You can do it, Della.*

"I accept your apology, but I need time. I'm not just going to jump into bed with you."

Oh dear God, that sounds so lame.

He pulls me closer to him until I can feel his body heat warming mine.

"Take all the time you need," he whispers against my cheek, and I swear this moment is so intense I can feel it between my legs, like a second heart beating.

He pulls slightly back until his mouth stops an inch from mine as if he's waiting for me to pull away.

My stomach tightens and my heart races. My insides turn to mush but I force myself to not close the distance between us. I need to be sure that he's not just saying these things, but that he actually means them.

"I should get you home," he whispers.

With all my strength I pull free from his arms.

"I like the rain. I'll walk. Have a good night, Carter."

Chapter 12

CARTER

I watch her walk away, sandals in her one hand.

I actually feel better now that I've had the chance to apologize. I'm not sure that she believes me, but at least I got to tell her how I feel.

I get in the car and slowly follow her home. There's no way I'm just going to leave her. Before she walks into the apartment block, she turns and waves at me.

I sit outside her building wishing I had her number.

I suck at dating. Hell, I've never dated a girl. I've never had to date any of them for them to spread their legs. Not that it's the reason I want to date Della. It's different with Della and it scares the living shit out of me.

The next morning I grab two coffees before heading over to Della's. So much for giving her time.

As I'm about to knock, the door swings open and Evie comes out.

"Hey, is Della home?"

"Yeah, be nice to her," she warns me before taking off.

I walk inside and shut the door behind me. When I walk into the living room, I freeze, drinking in the sight in front of me.

Della is lying upside down on the couch, with headphones on. She's bouncing her feet on the back of the couch, singing something about pixels and ratios.

I walk closer and standing next to her, I smile as I watch her. It takes her a few minutes to become aware of someone else in the room. Her eyes fly open and she scrambles up when she sees me.

Yanking the earphones off, a deep blush creeps up her neck.

"What are you doing here?"

"I brought you coffee. It's a little cold though."

She takes a cup and sips at it, her eyes wandering over my face as if she's searching for something.

"What are you thinking?" I hate not knowing where I stand with someone.

"You've been all dark and broody since I met you. You never gave me any signs that you were into me. Or I just completely missed them all. We don't even move in the same circles." Her honesty doesn't surprise me one bit. That's one of the things I like most about her.

"You think I'm broody? What, like the quiet, deep in thought kind, or the moping kind?" I smile at her. It feels weird not fighting with her. Not that I get some sadistic pleasure out of fighting, but because she's so damn feisty. I love seeing her eyes spark.

"The quiet kind," she says. "That's not the point I'm trying to make here."

"Okay, I'll keep quiet and listen," I laugh. "You're busy saying?"

I try to keep a straight face but for some reason, all I want to do is smile.

"Why are you really here, Carter?" Her voice is soft, not whisper soft, but rather a fragile kind of soft. It chips away at my heart because I know why. It's because she doesn't trust me and I can't blame her.

"I totally get how my sudden change of character must be confusing to you."

She nods as she makes herself more comfortable on the couch by tucking her legs beneath her.

"You've got that right. At least I knew where I stood with you when you hated me."

I shake my head as I sit down next to her. "I never hated you, Della. I hated myself for liking you, but I never hated you."

"Why?"

"I've never done the dating thing. I've never had to. Then I saw you and I actually thought about it for the first time. The night I brought Evie home, I couldn't wait to see if that spark was still there."

She sighs and whispers, "The night I laid into you."

"Yeah," I say as I lean my head back against the couch. "I was upset because of the things you said. What got to me most, was that I still liked you even after you insulted me. That pissed me off."

"I know that feeling," she says, placing her cup on the table next to the couch.

"We let it get out of hand, or at least, I did. The more I liked you, the more upset I got until," I wave towards her room, "the kiss on your bed."

"Carter," she says, her voice serious. I look at her and when I see the worry all over her face, I start to worry myself. What if she tells me to take a hike? I can't blame her if she does. "I have a lot going on in my life right now. I know I asked you for time, but the problem is there's no time. I'm busy with exams and I really need to focus all my attention on my studies. I'm too close to the end to mess it all up now."

"I know. You're right." All I can do is agree because she is right. I have my own exams to worry about.

"I don't want you to think that I'm shooting you down, because I'm not. I just can't think of us right now."

I get up, not wanting things to get even more awkward between us. I tried and my timing sucked.

She gets up and walks me to the door. She stands on her toes and presses a soft kiss to the corner of my mouth. I close my eyes, taking a deep breath of her scent.

"Thank you for understanding, Carter."

"Sure," I say, already walking away.

That's not what I had hoped for, but she gave me more than I deserved.

Well, that was the first and last that I try with a woman. From now on I'm sticking to screwing.

Della is just a whirlwind of confusing emotions.

Chapter 13

DELLA

I feel deflated as I walk out to the classroom where I just wrote my final exam.

I don't know what I expected my last day here to be like, but it wasn't this. Fireworks would've been nice. Hell, anything but this deserted silence.

I finished my last shift at Rameses on Tuesday. Yesterday I spent the whole day studying for today. Now I have to go pack. I want to be on the road first thing tomorrow morning.

I'll help Sue at the diner until Jamie's finished with school. We'll use the summer break to move to Raleigh, where I can enroll her in middle school.

When I walk into the apartment, I'm surprised to see the girls all here for a change. They're running between rooms, and there's a huge bundle of clothes on the couch.

"Are you all going home as well?" I ask as I eye the mess in the living room.

Evie comes hopping out of her room as she finishes slipping on a heel. She grabs my hand and pulls me in the direction of the couch.

"We're going to a party. They guys are having one last one to celebrate us all finishing our exams."

I start to shake my head, but then Willow joins in. "You're coming with."

Leigh comes out of the room, pulling a brush through her long blonde hair.

"We've lived together for three years, hardly spending time with each other. The party will be a nice way to say goodbye to each other and the guys."

She's got a point. I'd love to say goodbye to the guys, but mostly I'd love to see Carter one last time.

"Fine, let me just change into a clean pair of shorts and a shirt that doesn't smell like I was sweating through my final exam."

Willow steps in front of me and waves a hand at the couch. "Your usual shorts and t-shirt won't do for tonight."

I glance back at the couch and start to shake my head. "I'm not wearing a dress."

"You are and you're going to look gorgeous," Leigh says as she picks up something that looks more like a hairband than a shirt. Thankfully she tosses it to the side.

Soon Evie, Willow, and Leigh are digging through the heap of material, discussing what would make my ass look best.

They make me try on a dress that hardly covers my butt. I hardly have it on when I start to yank if off.

"I'm just going to wear some shorts," I say, rushing into my room. I grab one that I've made from a pair of old jeans I had lying around. I think it looks cute.

The girls seem to be happy with the shorts, but they won't let me wear any of my t-shirts. I'm told to wear a black bra as they shove a piece of chiffon in my hands. I shove my arms through the flimsy sleeves before trying to figure out what to do with the rest of it.

Evie takes the two long points and crossing them over my breasts she ties them at my back. The sleeves are wide and really pretty. The dark blue of the material matches my eyes, and I actually feel pretty. I finish the look off with some mascara.

I insist on taking my own truck. I'm not going to stay that late. I still need to pack most of my stuff before I leave early in the morning.

I follow behind Evie's Mini Cooper and when we pull up to the guys' house, I'm surprised to see that I've been walking by it every time on my way home from work.

Nervous excitement starts to bubble inside of me. I haven't seen Carter in almost two weeks. There were many moments I regretted telling him that the timing is wrong. A couple of times I almost asked Evie for his number. But I held out and finished my exams.

I take a deep breath and check my reflection in the review mirror. When I go home to Jamie, I'm going to have to be the adult. There won't be time for parties. For tonight I'm going to let my hair down.

There's a huge smile on my face as I cross the road and joining the girls. When I walk into the house, my eyes dart everywhere. It doesn't look like a frat house. It smells of expensive taste.

There are a lot of people already standing around. The girls all head in their own direction and I decide to go left. I walk into a huge room that opens up to a veranda and pool.

I smile as I watch everyone having fun. Some are dancing while others are swimming.

A girl with black hair and clear green eyes comes to stand next to me. We both stare at the people swimming.

"You look just out of place as I feel," she says.

I smile at her and nod. "I'm not used to parties." I reach a hand out to her. "I'm Della Truman."

She meets my smile as she takes my hand. "Mia Daniels. Do you know Rhett?"

I laugh, saying, "Who doesn't know Rhett?"

She nods in understanding. "Yeah, my older brother can be quite a handful."

My eyebrows pop up with surprise. "You're Rhett's sister?"

"Yeah. I deserve a gold medal for that."

I notice Logan by the pool where he's drying off. I wave and when I look back to Mia her eyes are glued to Logan.

I keep looking between the two as they stare at each other.

Taking Mia's hand I pull her outside with me. When we reach Logan I pull her a little forward so that she's closest to Logan.

"I've just met Mia," I say to break the silence before it becomes awkward.

"Yeah, she's spending the night here before we all head to New York."

The smile drops from my face. I knew this was goodbye, but New York? Deep down I was hoping I'd run into them somewhere down the line. That will never happen with them in New York.

Tonight is really the last time I'll see Carter.

"Have you seen Carter?" I ask as my heart starts to race. I'm going to make the most of tonight. I can't leave here with regrets.

"Yeah, I last saw him in the kitchen. Just head back in and take a right at the front door."

"Thanks." I rush through the people. Students keep coming in and the house is quickly filling up. It's going to be crazy soon. I have to find Carter before then.

When I find the kitchen, my eyes land on Carter. He takes a sip from his beer and laughs at something Marcus is saying.

A girl moves closer to him and she trails her finger down his bicep as she leans in. She's trying hard to get his attention. He glances at her but then his eyes meet mine and I see surprise registering on his face.

I gather every ounce of guts I have and I walk towards him.

He straightens to his full-length from where he was leaning against the counter.

When I reach him, the girl plasters herself against his side, clearly trying to show me that he belongs to her.

Chapter 14

CARTER

As I watch her walk towards me all I can think is that this has got to be a dream. One I don't want to wake from.

Della stops in front of me and scowls at the girl before she looks at me.

"Me or her?" Della says as if that's even an option.

I shove the girl away, never taking my eyes of Della.

"You," I growl as I slip my arm around her waist, pulling her body into mine.

Her hands crawl up my chest and when she reaches my jaw, she pulls me down to her. Our mouths crash into each other, sparking a scorching heat.

She tastes so damn sweet as her tongue brushes over mine. Instantly, I grow hard as her kiss grows more urgent.

Our tongues twist and when I nip at her bottom lip, I take hold of her ass and lift her body up against mine. She wraps her legs around me and I carry her out of the kitchen. Somehow I get us to my room without falling flat on my ass.

I lay her down on my bed and crawl over her, still not sure if this is just another dream I'm having of her. It's by far the best one.

She brings her one hand down to my chest. Our heated breathing is the only sound in the room as we devour each other.

She pushes me onto my back and for a second I'm confused until she follows, crawling on top of me.

Hell yes! I like where this is going.

She straddles me and a surge of frustration washes through me. I want the clothes gone. I want to feel Della skin to skin against me.

She pushes her hips down, rubbing her pussy against my cock. I can't wait to be buried deep inside of her. I want her so badly it will be over in a matter of seconds.

A soft moan slips from her lips and it's the hottest sound I've ever heard.

I pull myself up against the headboard and remove my shirt while I'm at it.

"This one, too," she whispers, tugging at the t-shirt I have on underneath. I let her pull it over my head. Delicious shivers rush over my skin as her fingers trace a hot path down my chest to my abs.

"What are you doing, Della?" I need to know what her intentions are, just how far she wants to take this.

"Second base for now." The two magic words fall hot against my jaw.

Her hips move again, rocking hard against me. We both groan and if she keeps pressing down on me like that, I'm going to detonate like a damn nuclear warhead. I grab hold of her hips with the intention of keeping her still but she has other ideas. She starts a slow and steady rhythm, rubbing her pussy hard against my hard as steel cock.

"Shit, Carter," she moans, her breaths coming faster.

Wanting to hear her moan again, I start placing kisses down her neck, working my way to her breasts. My mouth trails the curve of her breasts until I find her hard nipple through the material. I suck it into my mouth which earns me that sweet moan.

Her hands grip hold of my hair, and she arches her back, thrusting her breasts into my face. This night couldn't have worked out more perfect.

I need more of her. I kiss my way back up to her ear, placing a final kiss just below her earlobe.

"I want to touch you, Della. Dammit, I want you so much."

"Okay."

No fucking hesitation. I don't know what I did right to deserve this but there's no way I'm letting this chance slip through my fingers.

I untie the bow behind her but she has to help me get the thing off her. With the bra I need no help, and I have the thing off in a second.

My mouth actually waters at the sight of her firm breasts. I cup them both and caress her hard nipples with my thumbs. She's a perfect fit.

I roll her over until she's lying on her back. I grip hold of her shorts along with her panties, I drag them down her legs. It makes my insides turn to molten lava with want. I get rid of her sandals before I crawl back over her.

She's fucking naked beneath me. *Heaven.*

I trail hot kisses over her breasts, softly biting her creamy skin.

I place my hand on her hip, and it's heavenly to feel her bare skin beneath my fingertips. Shit, I want my clothes gone, but the second I remove my pants, it will be game over.

I lie down on top of her and rub myself against her center. Dry humping has never been such a turn on for me before.

"Do that ... do it again," she breathes hard. Her nails dig into my shoulders and she pulls me down to her mouth. I roll my hips against her again and it makes her body shudder underneath mine. Her tongue starts a fast and hot assault on me. Every nerve in my body is tingling. Every inch of me is on fire for her.

I slide my hand from her hip, and when my hand cups her, we both moan. Our mouths are inches from each other as I stare into her shining eyes.

I push a finger inside her, feeling how wet and hot she is for me. "Della, you're so ready," I groan.

She moves her hips up, pressing herself into my hand. She sucks in a deep breath, her movements becoming erratic with the lust building up between us.

"I've never …" she tries to speak when a low moan builds up in a throat. "Ah. Carter."

I rub my palm against her clit as I slip another finger inside her. She gasps sharply, her body tenses for a moment, and then a sweet tremble rocks her.

"Tell me if it hurts," I whisper. Because, shit, the last thing I want to do is hurt her.

"Uh-huh," she mumbles, then she brushes her cheek against mine, pressing soft kisses along my jaw.

I move my finger deeper inside of her, rubbing slow circles over her with my palm. She's so damn tight. It's going to feel like heaven to be inside of her.

She slides her hands to my sides and I take it as a good sign. I pull out slowly. When I thrust my fingers back in, deeper this time, her body arches into mine. She wraps her arms around my waist, clinging tightly.

"Ow." The one soft word makes me freeze.

"Ow, how?"

What the hell am I asking her?

"Uncomfortable." She takes a deep breath. "Keep going."

"We can stop." I start to pull away, but Della grabs hold of my wrist. Her head falls back against the pillow.

"Don't stop. I want this. Touch me, Carter." She presses my hand harder against her, forcing me back inside her, and it's so damn hot.

She doesn't have to ask me twice. I move slowly, checking her reaction. When she pushes up against my hand, I relax. I start gently, sliding my finger deeper with every thrust. Her breathing starts to pick up and she tightens her grip on my wrist.

"Is that better, babe?"

"So good," she breathes.

Her other hand finds its way along my abs, making a torturous path to my jeans. I feel her unbutton it and then the zipper goes next. She lets go of my wrist to yank my jeans away and pull my boxers back.

The second her fingertips brush the head of my erection, I almost come undone.

"Fucking hell, Della." I bury my face in her hair.

Every muscle in my body tightens as she grips me. This is more than I could ever ask for.

She starts her slow assault on me, working her hand up and down the length of me. The faster I thrust my fingers in and out of her, the quicker she strokes me.

"Carter, I'm gonna ..." she throws her head back. I know what she means. She has to stop or I'm going to come all over her.

I bring my other arm down between us and cover her hand, holding it still against me. Her body shudders, and when she opens her legs wider for me, I groan and quicken my pace.

"Ah, yes!"

She yanks her hands from my pants and covers my hand with both of hers, holding me to her as her breathing hitches. It's the most beautiful sound ever. Her movements slow down, and her hips start to do an erotic grind against me, as she rides out her orgasm.

"Carter," she whispers as the last of the trembles rakes through her body and I don't care. I reach over to the nightstand and grab a condom from the drawer.

I get rid of my pants and as I roll it over my cock, I drink in the sight of her flushed cheeks, and her hair splayed over the pillow all around her. I wish I could burn this image into my heart. I wish I could take this with me.

"I've never," I choke up and Della must hear the emotion in my voice because her eyes snap open. A faint blush creeps up her neck and colors her cheeks a perfect pink, God only knows what she's thinking now.

"I've never seen anyone more beautiful in my life," I finish what I wanted to say.

Her lips are swollen from the kisses and I reach up to brush my fingertips over them. Her eyes find mine as she sucks in a breath. Staring at each other, the air around us crackles with desire.

I want this woman to be mine. Not just for tonight, but forever. She challenges me like no one ever has.

"I've never dated before, Della, so I'm not sure what the right protocol is for dating. All I know is that I don't want casual with you. I want more. I want it all."

"We haven't even been on a date," she says. "We don't know each other."

I don't want her to panic right now. I place a tender kiss to her mouth and whisper, "I want you. I'll give you all the time you need to get to know me. I just want you to know that this is not just another screw, Della."

A sad smile forms around her lips, and it only makes me kiss her until it's gone.

"I'm a control freak. I want to make it clear that you're mine. I won't share. No matter what happens or how long it takes for us to get to know each other, you need to know that you're mine."

Her eyes dance over my face as if she's trying to make sure whether I'm being serious right now.

"So you're one of those men with alpha tendencies?"

"And I get jealous. I'm an only child. Sharing is not in my DNA."

"No one has ever gotten jealous over me before. It's kind of hot."

She reaches for me and I let her pull me down against her. I can't believe I wasted so much time by being such an asshole to her. We could have had this so much sooner.

Chapter 15

DELLA

This night is turning out to be perfect. Carter seriously just rocked my world.

I don't give him time to say something else. I reach up and pull him back down on top of me. I can actually hear every beat of my heart as nervous anticipation builds up inside of me.

I'm conscious of everything about this moment, the way his body is pressing into mine in all the right places. The carnal growls he makes when I touch him unravels me.

His mouth devours mine making my mind cloud over with lust for him. I want this moment to last forever. I slide my hands down his back, tracing his spine until I reach his ass, where I let my hands linger.

He presses his body harder down on mine, his chest firm against my breasts. I feel him hard and ready between my legs. My abdomen clenches as my legs fall open for him.

"Fucking perfect," he groans.

I trail hot kisses along his jaw as he positions himself at my opening.

I know that I'm taking a huge risk, putting all I've worked so hard for on the line, but I can't stop now.

Am I being selfish? *Yes.*

But, I want this so much. Just this one moment with Carter before we have to say goodbye. A passion filled moment made up of sweet lies. I want something that will be just mine that I'll be able to cherish and remember forever.

"You're the one, Della," he whispers, as he starts to slowly push inside of me.

I kiss him harder, and as he slowly fills me all I feel is a slight discomfort. When he pulls out, I sigh with pleasure and practically melt against him.

Carter slips his arms under me, crushing my body to his.

"I knew you were mine from the second I saw you," he says, as he rolls his hips into me, making tiny firecrackers explode everywhere inside of me, I feel every delicious, hard inch of him.

My mouth drops open. I can't even get a sound out as Carter shows me a whole new level of ecstasy.

He's ruining me. I'll never be the same again.

A quickening feeling builds in my abdomen, and I dig my fingers into his ass, trying to keep him there.

A low moan escapes my throat and I throw my head back, pushing my body into his, trying to get closer still, as he rocks into me.

He moves his hand to my butt and keeps me locked to him. I didn't even notice I was moving. His hand holding me in place is exactly what I need because I feel him so much deeper as he starts to thrust harder.

He speeds up and with every powerful push of his hips, he drives his cock inside me. Tingles start in my toes, and my body turns to liquid ecstasy as I clench and contract with one wave of pure deliciousness after the other.

I can't moan. I can't breathe until the last ripple ebbs away, and I feel Carter shudder as he's overcome with pleasure above me.

His eyes are burning like twin coals, alive with passion. He's so beautiful that it makes my insides quiver. I can't believe I just had sex with Carter Hayes.

Damn. That was amazing.

Tears well up in the back of my throat because this moment is so perfect that I don't want to give it up. I want to be selfish and stay here with him.

I reach up and trace my fingers down the side of his face. He places a chaste kiss on my lips.

"Be right back." I miss his warmth the second he pulls away from me. He gets out of bed and walks to the toilet.

When he closes the door behind him, I sit up and look around me.

The sheets are crumpled around me and the smell of sex hangs heavy in the air.

His phone starts to ring somewhere in the room. He comes out of the toilet and quickly pulls on his jeans. Fishing the phone from his pocket, he looks down at the screen. I catch a glimpse of the phone and see the name Charlotte.

He moves away from the bed as he answers it.

I hear a high-pitched voice on the other side.

Carter gives me an awkward smile and walks to the door. He's just about to pull it shut behind him when I hear him say, "You're not interrupting anything. What's up?"

That's when I realize all his words were lies. Empty lies and I fell for each of them. He just won the bet. I let him have me for four hundred dollars.

Humiliated, I get dressed. I struggle with the stupid shirt I was wearing, and grab one of his instead. I slip my sandals on and rush out of the room.

"Just stay calm. I'll leave right now," I hear him say and the words just make everything so much clearer. I was just a screw.

I run down the hallway and rush down the stairs and out of the house.

I get in my truck and break all the speed limits to get back to the apartment.

When I run into my room, the tears start to fall.

I'm an idiot.

I throw my belongings in my bags and take everything down to my truck. When I'm done packing everything I remove my key from my keychain. I close the front door and lock it, before shoving the key under the door.

If I hurry I can be back in Saluda before midnight.

Chapter 16

CARTER

When I see Charlotte's name flashing on my screen, I know it can't be good. She's been Dad's PA and right hand for so long she might as well be family.

I don't want to have this conversation in front of Della, so I step out of my room as I answer.

"Can you talk," she says hurriedly, not giving me time to greet her.

"You're not interrupting anything. What's up?"

"You need to catch the first flight back home. It's your Dad."

Ice cold fear washes over me. I shove a hand through my hair as my heart starts to race with dread.

"What about Dad? What happened?"

"Come home!" she screams. "He's had another heart attack. They say it's bad. You need to come right now."

It feels as if my life is shattering around me.

"Just stay calm. I'll leave right now," I say automatically.

As I cut the call Rhett comes up the stairs. He looks pissed off until he sees my face.

"What happened? Della just ran out of here upset about something. Did you have another fight?"

I shake my head, not understanding what he's saying.

"Dad had a heart attack," I say as I'm being sucked under by the delayed shock.

"Fuck. Is he okay?"

Rhett takes hold of my shoulder and I force the words out. "We have to go home. It's bad."

"Pack your shit. I'll get rid of everyone and book our flights."

I turn to walk back into my room, but Rhett pulls me back and gives me a hug.

"He's a fighter."

I nod as apprehension flood me. It feels as if the night is closing on me and I won't get to see the sun shine again.

"I can't lose him," I say more to myself than to anyone else.

Chapter 17

DELLA

NINE MONTHS LATER.

It feels as if the pain is going to tear right through me. The medication they gave me isn't helping at all.

"Please," I groan through another contraction. "Give me anything to take the pain away."

"Just breathe," Sue says as she wipes the beading sweat from my forehead. The nurse said the doctor will be here soon. He'll give you something."

"I want something now," I cry miserably. How the hell did my mother do this twice?

The nurse comes back into the room. Sue glares at her, concern etched between the lines on her face. "Will the doctor be here before the baby comes?"

"This is normal, ma'am. The doctor will be here in time," she assures us, but it's not what I want to hear.

"Nothing about this is normal," She shrieks. "She doesn't pop out a baby every other day. This is a very overwhelming moment for the child, and painful. Go fetch the doctor now."

The nurse quickly leaves promising she'll get the doctor.

"Thank you," I groan. I hold Sue's hand tighter as the next contraction starts.

She smiles motherly at me, wiping my face with a cool cloth.

We've been through hell in the last nine months. We almost lost Sue to pneumonia. I took over running the diner while she was recovering and the last month, she's been taking care of me.

Shortly after I got home, I started to get sick. Soon after that, we found out I was pregnant. I had to give up on my dream of moving to Raleigh.

I got something else in return though – a family. We might not have much, but Sue has made sure that we will always have enough. With her and Jamie's help, we've converted my room into a nursery for the baby.

The nurse returns with the anesthesiologist. "Just a few more seconds and the pain will be gone."

I nod as I breathe through the intense pain pulsing in my abdomen.

He works behind me as he inserts something into my spine, and after a few minutes, I feel much better. I'm a little nauseous but at least the pain is only a dull ache now.

We have to wait another two hours before the nurse returns with Dr. Lee. He looks tired which isn't very comforting.

"Della, when I tell you to, I want you to push," he says.

I nod again, just wanting this all to be over with.

"Push," he instructs.

After long minutes of pushing, I slump back against the bed. I can't do this. It's too hard.

I start to cry but then Sue squeezes my hand. "Honey, you can do this. You're so strong. Bring this baby into the world." She keeps rubbing my hand, her eyes shining with tears.

I've never seen Sue so emotional in my life.

"The baby is crowning, "Dr. Lee says. "Push hard, Della."

I cry silently as I push with everything I have. When a cry fills the room, I start to sob. It's the most beautiful sound I've ever heard.

"It's a girl," Dr. Lee says.

When I look at Sue, tears are streaming down her face. There's an astonished smile on her face as she looks at the baby.

"Are you ready, Mom," The nurse says and my eyes dart to the bundle in her arms.

She lays her down in my arms, and I drink in the little red face. She has a mop of dark hair, just like Carter.

"Do you have a name?" the nurse asks.

I shake my head, not sure if there is a name out there to do her justice.

"Daniele," I whisper. "After Mom."

Sue smiles proudly. "It's a good name, strong, too."

"We'll complete the birth certificate for you. Who should we list under the father?"

I almost blurt out no one, but that would not be fair to Daniele.

"Carter Hayes."

Chapter 18

CARTER

THREE YEARS AFTER THE BIRTH OF DANIELE.

I walk down the main road to meet up with the rest of the gang for lunch.

Finally, I got some time off from my busy schedule. The last four years have been a fucking nightmare. After Dad passed away, I had to step in and fill his shoes. There was so much to learn and I would've caved under all the pressure if it weren't for the guys. They kept my head above water.

I walk into the only diner in this small town and spot the guys sitting at the biggest table in the back. I don't know how the guys found this place but apparently they have great outdoor activities.

"Hey, guys, thanks for waiting for me," I say as I take my seat."

"Did the conference call go well?" Rhett asks. He passes me a menu and I start to look over the dishes.

"Yeah, Charlotte will handle things from here on out. So we better make the most of this week. There won't be an opportunity like this for a long while after I get back to the office."

"Sir, do you wanna eat?" a tiny voice asks next to me.

I look down and see a pretty girl with dark curls staring up at me. She's got bright blue eyes.

"Daniele." An older girl takes hold of the little girl's hand and tries to pull her away from our table.

"No," Daniele wines and she stomps her tiny feet on the floor. "I wanna help."

"It's okay," I say.

"Daniele, come here," another voice says and this time the little girl listens.

I watch her run to a woman. She crouches down to catch the little girl. When she looks up my heart stutters and a wave of pain hits hard. My pulse starts to race as the whole table grows quiet.

"Fuck." I hear Rhett breathe in shock.

Slowly, I rise from the chair and I walk closer to her. My eyes dance between her and the little girl.

Finally, I manage to find my voice. "Della," I breathe her name.

It's been four years. She just vanished. After I buried Dad, I heard that she had left that same night. None of the girls or guys had her number. She broke what was left of my fucking heart. I lost my Dad and Della in one night.

"Carter," she whispers. Her face is pale and it makes the blue of her eyes pop.

The teenage girl comes to stand next to Della and I notice that they all three have the same color eyes.

"Are they your sisters?" I ask just to try and make some kind of conversation.

It's fucked up that I know every inch of her body but I don't really know anything about her.

"Um," she takes a shaky breath and turns to the teenage girl. "Take Daniele to the back."

She waits until they're gone before she turns back to me. "Jamie is my sister. Daniele is my daughter."

Fuck, she's married. The thought shudders through me. Even after all these years I've had a flicker of hope that I'd run into to her again, and that we would get the chance we never had.

"Wow, when did you get married?" I ask, swallowing down the heavy disappointment.

She shakes her head. "I didn't." She even holds up her left hand for me to see. No ring.

I frown, not happy with the fact that someone got her pregnant before putting a ring on her finger.

"Where's the father?"

Yeah, even after all these years, I'll kick a guy's ass if he hurts her.

She just shakes her head. "We're busy with the lunch rush. Can we meet up later?"

I look around the place and see that it is packed with people. "You work here?"

It's another surprise. Why would she work in a diner when she has a degree?

"Once a waitress, always a waitress," she says.

I can see that she's in a hurry, but I want to make sure we meet up later. "I'm staying at The Falls. Can we meet there?"

"Sure. I'll come by after we close. It should be around ten."

"Great." I watch her walk away before I take my seat again.

Chapter 19

DELLA

I keep watching the time. It feels as if I'm on death row.

Sue passed away last year. She left us everything, but it hasn't helped. At first, I kept breaking even at the end of every month, but things have slowly been getting worse.

At the rate things are going I'm not going to be able to keep this place up and running for much longer. I feel the familiar grip of panic wrap its claws around my heart. How am I going to provide for Danny and Jamie?

I also have Carter to worry about now. Once I've told him that Daniele is our daughter, he might try to take her from me. He has money and I don't.

Fuck.

I rub my temples, trying to get rid of the headache hammering behind my eyes.

Why can't something go my way for once? Why does life have to be so hard?

Jamie took Danny up to bed after the dinner rush. She said she would watch her while I go talk to Carter.

I lock up and slowly walk up the road. The town is always buzzing with life over the summer holidays but the rest of the year it's dead. People love the outdoor activities we offer in Saluda. I was hoping the summer wave of visitors would help me save the diner, but it's going to take a miracle for that to happen.

When I reach the hotel, Carter is staying at I stop to wipe my palms on my shorts.

I feel like crawling into the nearest hole and crying. I never thought I'd see him again. Out of all the holiday destinations, why did he come to this one?

As I step into the foyer, I'm surprised to see Carter sitting on one of the couches near reception. When he sees me, he stands up. His eyes lock on mine and I feel the wave of intensity all the way from across the room. The last four years have shaped him into a determined man. His shoulders are square and strong under the power of wealth that rests on them

Forcing myself to move forward, I meet him in the middle. I'd rather run and hide, but that's not an option right now.

"I didn't tell you which room was mine," he says. "Let's go up. We'll have more privacy there."

Following him, all I can think is that no one will be there to bear witness when he kills me.

We get in the elevator and I watch the numbers flick over as we go higher. Off course he'll be on the top floor.

I knew he came from a wealthy family before we had sex. Afterwards, I found out just how wealthy he was. When his dad died it was all over the news. Carter is now the CEO of the largest publishing house in America. I used to dream about working at Indie Ink Publishers. That's why I studied Graphic Design. I would've gotten a good job in Raleigh and worked my way to New York.

Would've. It was just a pipe dream.

Carter opens the door and waits for me to walk into the suite before he follows. I hear the door click shut while my eyes take in all the wealth around me.

Just one of the paintings on the wall alone must cost more than everything I own.

"Can I pour you something to drink?" he asks as he makes his way over to the bar.

I shake my head and again wipe my hands on my shorts. "I'm sorry about your Dad," I say. "I saw on the news that he passed."

He just smiles at me, and then asks casually, "How have you been?"

I watch him pour amber liquid into a heavy looking crystal glass.

We're from opposite worlds. I should've seen it back then, but I was too in love.

Now it's all I see. Every difference between us forms a solid wall we'll never be able to break down.

The thought that hurts most is knowing he can take Daniele from me, and there will be nothing I can do to stop him.

I don't understand why he's come here after all this time. I sent him letters after Daniele was born but he didn't care back then.

"Why did you come here?" I finally ask. I can't hide from what's to come so I might as well face it head on.

Chapter 20

CARTER

My hand freezes on the whiskey glass and my eyes snap up to meet hers.

I didn't expect hostility. I didn't expect anything but two friends catching up on old times.

"I'm here for a short vacation. The guys want to go down the white water rapids."

She frowns and I see confusion flash over her face. She's still breathtakingly beautiful and her eyes still have the power to knock me on my ass.

"You're only here for vacation?" Her confusion quickly makes way for hurt.

Is she actually hurt that I'm not here for her? Up until a few hours ago I didn't know where she was or what happened to her. Fuck, it's not like she gave me a choice back then. She decided we were over before we even had a chance to start.

"I didn't know you lived in Saluda."

When anger starts to spark in her eyes, I step out from behind the bar.

"What's with the aggressive behavior? You're the one that snuck out of my room without so much as a thanks for the fuck."

Her lips part and she inhales sharply. "Snuck out of your room?" she seethes, clearly pissed off.

This is quickly going from awkward to insane.

"Charlotte," she spits the word at me.

I give her a look of warning. I won't have her drag my PA into this.

"I left because of Charlotte. I stayed away because of your precious Charlotte. She made it pretty clear that a gold digger like me wouldn't be getting a dollar from you."

"What the fuck are you talking about?" I take a huge gulp of whiskey, needing to feel the burn down my throat.

"Don't play dumb with me. Charlotte phoned and you couldn't get away from me fast enough. You won the bet. You screwed me for four hundred dollars. After she was born I tried to contact you three times. Twice my letters came back return to sender. The third one Charlotte answered, warning me that she would destroy everything I held dear if I tried to contact you again. I backed off. I did as she asked. Now you're here." She gasps for breath between sentences before she goes on. "I don't have much for her to destroy, so I'm begging you, please leave."

I let her words sink in first, thinking them over. Nothing she's saying is making any sense.

"You've been in contact with my PA?" I ask to make sure we're talking about the same Charlotte.

She nods and taking a step closer to me, her voice cracks when she says, "Please, Carter. I don't want anything from you. Just let us be. I'm begging you."

I frown down at her, not understanding a word she's saying. Fuck, she might as well be speaking a different language.

"Why did you write to me? Why didn't you come see me or try to phone me?"

She throws her hands in the air, a look of frustration clouding her features. "I couldn't travel to New York with a newborn. Besides, I didn't have that kind of money. My truck would never make the trip. Every time I tried to call you, they would tell me that you're not accepting any calls. It's hard to phone such a huge company and to demand they put me through to their CEO."

"You just left, Della. Why did you try to contact me anyway?"

For a moment she just stares at me but then all the blood drains from her face. I move forward when it looks like she's going to faint.

"You really don't know," she whispers hauntingly.

"Sit down," I snap. Luckily she listens and she takes a seat on the couch. I sit down beside her and place the glass on the table.

"I don't know what?" I ask, hoping that the next thing out of her mouth will actually make sense.

"Daniele," she whispers.

"Your daughter? What does she have to do with …" It hits me like a lightning bolt.

I stand up and move away from her as shock ripples over me.

"Daniele Hayes," she says as tears spill over her cheeks.

I have a child.

The shock is quickly joined by anger.

I have a beautiful little girl and she's been kept from me.

Chapter 21

DELLA

"I have a child and you didn't tell me?" he spits the words out like they taste bitter.

"What?" I hiss, not believing what I'm hearing right now. "Why didn't I tell you? Are you being serious right now? Haven't you heard a word I've been saying?"

He stares darkly at me. Suddenly he moves, and he throws the glass against the wall. The shattering sound echoes through the room along with my thundering heart.

I forgot how cruel Carter can be. He stalks up and down, every moment he makes is filled with rage.

Fear slithers down my spine as I slowly get up. When he doesn't make a move for me, I run for the door. I yank it open, but Carter is right behind me. His arms darts past me and he slams the door shut. I press up against the wood closing my eyes. Why did I think I would actually be able to have a normal conversation with him?

Keeping his hand against the door, he presses his chest against my back. I can feel every hard muscle and I flatten my body against the door. I feel his hot breath on my neck and it sends shivers racing through my body.

Even after all these years, my body has a mind of its own when it comes to Carter Hayes.

"I'm not going to hurt you. Let's both just calm down, okay," he whispers.

I nod quickly. He moves back and I turn around so I can at least see him.

"I'm sorry I threw the glass. I'm just so fucking upset right now." He looks at me and I nod again. "Don't look at me like that, Della. I've never hit a woman and I won't start now. I just want clarity on what the hell happened four years ago."

"Okay," I say but I don't move away from the door. He has done nothing to earn my trust.

"You said that you tried to contact me?" He genuinely looks confused. Could it be that he didn't know anything about the letters?

"Yes, the letters that Charlotte responded to. I really tried to get in touch with you. I wanted you in Daniele's life. She needs a father. I'd never be that cruel to my own daughter to keep her from her dad."

"I can't wrap my mind around Charlotte being involved. She's just my PA. Why the hell would she keep news of my own child from me?"

I shake my head. That's something I can't answer for him. He sits down on the couch and I decide to cautiously approach him. When he seems calm, I sit down next to him.

My eyes wander over his strong features. He was attractive in college, but now that he's become a man and a powerful CEO, he's disturbingly handsome.

"She's three?" he asks. When he makes eye contact a piece of my heart breaks for him. Tears are shimmering in his eyes. I've never seen Carter so vulnerable.

"Yes. She's healthy, Carter. I really did my best. She never went without food and I always made sure she was warm. I promise."

He grinds his teeth and the action makes me sit back.

He reaches for my hand and gives it a squeeze, then he breaks down right before my eyes. I place my other hand over his, not knowing what I can do to make this easier for him. I can't imagine how he must feel.

He covers his eyes with his other hand and cries. I can't keep my own tears back as I scoot closer to him. I pull him into my arms and hold him. I would also be heartbroken if I found out that I missed the first three years of my daughter's life.

Tears roll down my cheeks as all the heartache of the past few years overwhelms me.

"I'm sorry I wasn't there," he whispers when he's regained some control over his emotions. "I want to see her, Della. I want to hold my little girl."

"You will. It's late and she's sleeping. If you come over tomorrow morning before the diner opens, you can spend some time with her."

"I have to contact my attorney."

His words shock me. I didn't expect to hear them. I thought we would work things out between ourselves. *I was stupid.*

I get up and wring my hands nervously. "I can't fight you for her, Carter. You know that. I'm all she's known the past three years. Don't do that to our little girl. I'm her mother. Please, don't take her from me." I gasp for air as a sob rips through me. I'll die. I'll just cease to exist.

When he just stares at me, I start to ramble. "She's only three, Carter. Her biggest achievement is when she sleeps through the night without wetting the bed."

He stands up and takes hold of my shoulders. "I'm not going to take her from you, Della. I'm not a fucking monster and I'm not the enemy. I need my attorney so he can get a DNA test done. He needs to get behind what role Charlotte plays in all of this. I need to make sure Daniele is taken care of, should something happen to me. I'm just going to do for her what my dad did for me. It's all things I have to think of right now."

I focus on one thing only. "You're not taking her from me?"

"No. We'll share custody. She needs both of us."

I start to laugh and throw my arms around his neck. I give him a tight hug but soon my laughter turns into a sobbing mess. His arms fold around me and he holds me tightly to him as I cry my heart out against his chest.

"Thank you," I manage to whisper.

He pulls back and frames my face with his strong hands. "Thank you," he says with tears shimmering in his eyes. "You gave me a child, Della." He presses a kiss to my forehead.

It's been one hell of a night and I know it's far from over. But for now, I feel a sense of relief knowing that my child is still safe with me.

Chapter 22

CARTER

As soon as I close the door behind Della I phone Rhett.

The second he answers the phone, I growl, "I need you to come to my room."

"Yes boss," he growls back. He only calls me boss when I piss him off.

Since Dad passed away, the guys have been looking at me to fill his shoes. Dad took them all in during our high school years. We didn't give him much of a choice. He once told me that I have a strong group of friends, something he wished he had growing up. That's why he treated them like his own. It was just another way he ensured my future.

The guys all joined me in the company. We're looking at going worldwide in the next year. If I can secure a deal with the largest publishing house in Europe then Indie Ink Publishing will be unbeatable. That was Dad's dream and I'm going to make sure it happens.

While I'm waiting for Rhett, I phone George, my attorney. I quickly bring him up to speed with what I need before I let the man turn in for the night. Logan is training under George so he can take over from the old man when he retires.

Rhett comes in just as I phone Logan.

"It's midnight and I'm on vacation," Logan growls as he answers the phone.

"I just spoke to George so he'll handle things. Della told me that Daniele is mine. I told George to get a DNA test done. If she's really mine then we need to set something in place to protect her."

"Fuck," Logan groans. "I'll start on it first thing in the morning."

"Thanks." I throw the phone on the couch and start to stalk up and down again. I've never felt so restless in my life.

"What happened?" Rhett asks. He picks up my phone and drops it on the table before he stretches out on the couch.

"Daniele is mine. That little girl from the diner is mine."

Rhett sits back up, but he doesn't look surprised. "I saw that one coming the second I saw her in Della's arms."

"Of course. I keep forgetting you're all-fucking-knowing," I growl at him.

"Don't be pissed off at me. It's your cock that got her pregnant."

I take a deep breath so I don't lose my shit with my best friend.

"She said she wrote to me, that Charlotte threatened her to stay away," I grind the words out.

"Well, think about it. Did you tell Charlotte about Della?"

"Of course not. It had nothing to do with my fucking PA!"

"Calm your tits, man. I know this is all a shock to you, but you need to stay calm or you're going to fuck this all up. The point I'm trying to make is that Charlotte had no way of knowing that Della was the

147

real thing. The woman has to deal with all your fan mail. I'm sure there are a lot of women out there claiming that you're the father of their kid. This kind of thing happens when you have money."

I wipe tiredly over my face. "You're right."

I once got a call from a guy that threatened to kill his family if I didn't give him ten thousand dollars. That was the only time I answered Charlotte's phone. Things got so busy I forgot about it. How many calls like that does she get?

"I don't know what to do."

"Right now you need to get some sleep. Tomorrow we'll figure it all out. One thing you have to keep in mind is that you can't make any decisions about that kid without thinking of Della. You fucked up four years ago. Don't fuck up again."

I glare at him as he leaves but I know he's right.

I'm heading for a shit storm of epic proportions.

One thing is certain, if that DNA test proves that Daniele is mine, there is no way I'm leaving this town without her.

Chapter 23

DELLA

"I wanna wear the pink ones," Danny says for the hundredth time.

I didn't sleep much last night and I'm trying to be patient with her. "You wore it yesterday, Danny. It's dirty. Wear your purple socks."

She crosses her arms over her chest, her bottom lip starts to tremble and she looks absolutely heartbroken. "I want my pink ones," she whispers as the first fat tear rolls down her cheek.

Just then there's a knock at the door. "Jamie will you let Carter in, please," I ask as I sit down on the floor in front of Danny.

Jamie looks at me, then Daniele, before she walks to the front of the diner. I haven't had time to talk to her yet. I haven't had time to absorb the past twenty-four hours, let alone try making sense of it.

"I'll make you a deal. I'll wash them tonight so you can wear them tomorrow." She shakes her head, pushing her bottom lip out even further.

Jamie kneels next to me. Taking the purple socks from me she says, "Princess Danny has a visitor. Let's get these socks on so you see who it is."

Danny forgets about sulking and lets Jamie put the socks on. It's times like this I feel like a failure.

I stand up and pulling my ponytail a little tighter, I turn, but I'm stopped in my tracks by the look on Carter's face. His eyes are filled with worry as they lock with mine.

Dammit! He just saw how I couldn't even get socks on his daughter's feet.

"I'm a princess," Danny starts to sing. She starts to spin around so her dress fans out around her.

Carter crouches down and slowly a smile spreads over his face. His eyes are glued to his little girl. I can see that he's fighting to hold himself back.

"Danny," I say as I kneel beside her again.

She stops spinning and gulps in huge amounts of air. "That was a lot of work."

I take her hand and pull her tiny body closer to mine. I don't know how to introduce her to her father, so I just spit the words out. "This is Carter Hayes."

Her little face lights up and suddenly she's very interested in Carter. "Hey, that's my name. You can't have the same name, silly."

Carter sucks in a harsh breath of air and tears start to well in his eyes.

"You're my little girl," he whispers as he struggles to keep control over his emotions.

Daniele's eyes go wide and she looks from me to him. She pulls away from me and walks right up to Carter. She places her tiny hand on his shoulder. "Shh, it's okay. Don't cry. You can have the same name."

A sob shudders through him and he grabs her to him. He buries his face in her dark curls.

I cover my mouth with a trembling hand when she hugs him back. She pats him and gently brushes her hand over his hair. "It's okay," she whispers.

I take a deep breath and get up. I walk closer to them and placing my hand on her back, I get her attention.

"Daniele, this is your daddy."

She pulls away and her tiny hands cradle his face. "I have a daddy?"

I can't hold it in anymore. I get up and turn away from them as the tears burst free.

"Yeah, I'm your daddy," he says.

"Where did you come from?" she asks with all the innocence in the world.

Quickly, I wipe the tears from my face and I turn back to them. I can see the lost look on his face. He has no answer for her.

"Your daddy had to fight a dragon so he could come save his princess," Jamie suddenly says.

I've never loved my sister more than I do in this moment.

Carter looks at Jamie from over Danny's head and he mouths thank you.

"You're a king?" Danny asks.

Carter nods and smiles at her with all the love only a father can have for his little girl. "Yeah."

"Is mommy your queen? Are you going to get married? I want a pink dress, Daddy," she says with a serious look on her face.

Carter picks her up as he rises to his full length. "I'll buy you all the pink dresses you want, but first I have to talk to your mommy, okay."

Danny sighs heavily. "Okay."

He presses a kiss to her chubby cheek before he reluctantly hands her over to Jamie.

"I want pink milk," she says to Jamie as they walk to the kitchen.

Chapter 24

CARTER

"She's going through a pink phase right now," Della says as she nervously starts to play with her watch.

"Is it okay if we talk here?" I ask.

"Sure, let's sit at one of the tables."

I follow her to the nearest one and pull a chair out for her to sit. When I've taken a seat myself, I say, "I spoke with Rhett last night and with Charlotte this morning. The reason she ignored your letter is because she gets constant demands that I'm someone's father and that I should pay up. She dealt with your letter the same way she dealt with all the others."

"But I wasn't making any demands. I just wanted you to know," Della quickly starts to defend herself.

"I know," I sigh. "I never told Charlotte about you. There was no way for her to know who you really were."

"Oh." Della slumps back in her chair and her eyes drop to her hands. "I suppose it makes sense with me just being a one night stand."

I cross my arms over my chest and frown at her. "If my memory serves me correctly, I was the one who fucking spilled my guts all over the place and you were the one who just walked over it."

"What?" she breathes.

"I made it pretty fucking clear that I wanted more. I was ready to give you the fucking world and you just walked away from it."

"You're still an alpha asshole!" she hisses at me.

She actually just fucking hissed at me.

"Don't fucking hiss at me," I growl.

"Don't accuse me of things I didn't do!" she shrieks. "And don't growl at me."

Anger takes over and I stand up. "Don't tell me what to do. No one fucking tells me what to do."

"Guys," Jamie suddenly snaps from the entrance that leads to the back. "There's a little girl in there that can hear all of this." She looks to Della. "Shit happened and you need to get over it. Danny is all that matters right now." Then her eyes fall on me and somehow this teenage girl has the power to make me feel ten inches small. "You're not some big shot CEO here. You're just a father and you need to start acting like one. You can't use that language around her."

Jamie walks up to me and holds out her hand. "Money, please. I'll take your daughter out to buy something pink while you rip each other apart."

Guilt washes over me as I give her one of my credit cards.

"What do you expect me to do with this?"

Fuck, this girl has balls.

"Swipe it," I grind the words out. "If my little girl wants something then you fucking swipe the card."

She grabs the card from my hand but instead of walking away, she takes another step closer to me. She only reaches my shoulder but that doesn't intimidate her.

"You will never talk to me like that again. I'm your daughter's aunt. I changed your daughter's diapers instead of getting sleep for my exams. I filled your shoes and you will respect me for that."

Once again, she's put me nicely in my place. "You're right. I'm sorry. Thank you, Jamie. It might not mean much now but I'll make it up to you."

"I want nothing from you," she says, her face pulling with disgust. "Just be the father my niece needs."

$$\infty\infty\infty\infty$$

I got the results yesterday. There's not a doubt that Daniele is mine.

Today will be the first day that I'll be alone with Daniele. I walk into the dinner and go look for Della. I find her in a make shift office of some sort. Her shoulders are hunched forward as she looks through some papers.

"Hi," I say so she'll know I'm here.

"My heart!" She swings around and sends some papers flying from the desk.

I start to pick them up when my eye catches the red words stamped in bold over the one letter. *Final notice.*

I see two more like the one I'm holding before Della manages to gather them all.

"Are you in financial trouble?" I ask as she takes the letter I'm holding.

She doesn't even look at me. "I'll manage."

"We need to talk about all of this," I snap and I take a step closer to her.

"Talk about what?" Her eyes snap up to finally meet mine.

"I'm leaving in three days, Della."

"Oh." She sits down again and shoves all the papers to the side. "We need to schedule some sort of visiting thing. "

I shake my head. "No. When I leave here Daniele goes with me."

Della darts to her feet and all the blood drains from her face. Her breathing starts to speed up until it looks like she's going to faint.

"Hey, take a breath." I put my arm around her and her hands fist in my shirt.

She leans her forehead against my chest. "You said you wouldn't take her from me."

I frame her face with my hands and force her to look up at me.

"I'm not taking her from you. You have a choice, Della. Come with."

Confusion washes over her face but she doesn't look any calmer.

"I can't just leave Saluda. Jamie is about to start her sophomore year. What about the diner?"

"What about your parents?" I ask, not understanding what Jamie has to do with all of this.

Della takes a breath and shakes her head. "We never talked about our families."

She massages her temples tiredly and it makes me want to hold her. After all this time, I still care about this woman.

"Jamie is my responsibility. Our dad died when we were young and our mother died my sophomore year. The only reason I could go study was because of Sue, but she passed away last year. The diner used to be hers."

Listening to her I once again realize that I know so little about her.

"Obviously Jamie will come with. I'll put her in a good school."

She shakes her head and laughs bitterly. "You can't solve everything in life by throwing money at it."

"Fuck, Della. Can you give me a break? At least I'm trying."

She still has the gift of pissing me off in a split-second.

"I'm sorry," she whispers. She looks down at her feet.

I glance down and notice that the strap of her one sandal is stapled down. I let my eyes go over her, really taking in the sorry state of her clothes. I'm sure I saw her wearing this exact outfit in college. There are dark circles under her eyes and she's too thin.

"How bad are things really? I'm not going to take Daniele away from you. I just want to help."

She covers her face with both her hands and whispers, "I can't hold it together anymore. Nothing I do works. Everything just keeps getting worse. They're going to close the diner in thirty days. We live upstairs. I just … I can't."

I pull her into my arms and hold her to my chest. She's been suffering all along and not once has she asked me for anything but to not take Daniele from her. This is what made me fall in love with her the first time. She's so strong.

Keeping one arm around her, I pull slightly away. I place a finger under her chin and nudge her face up. Her beautiful blue eyes are drowning in worry.

"Let me help."

She nods and when she tries to take a step back, I tighten my hold on her. There's confusion on her face when she looks up at me again.

"I'll have my attorney close the diner and settle the debt, to keep you from being declared bankrupt."

She starts to shake her head again and when she opens her mouth, I quickly cover it with my hand.

"Just listen before you lose your shit. There's nothing for you here, Della. You have a fucking degree. Why are you still waitressing? Let's pack it all up. The three of you come with me. You can work at Indie Ink and pay me back every fucking cent if that will make you feel better. Think of Daniele. Think of Jamie. You can't even take care of yourself never mind two kids. It's time to let go of all of this. It's time for a change."

When I move my hand away from her mouth, she asks, "Why would you do all that for us?"

"You're the mother of my child, Della. Jamie is Daniele's aunt. You're my family. Why the fuck wouldn't I take care of my own."

Finally, she nods and it feels like I can breathe for the first time. "Only if you let me pay you back. I want it on paper."

"I'll have Logan draw it up."

161

Chapter 25

DELLA

"Oh, wow," Jamie breathes as we walk into our new apartment. "Let's go find your room, Danny."

Wow is the understatement of the damn year. I glare at all the expensive stuff while I wait for Jamie and Danny to leave the huge living room.

"This was not part of the deal," I snap at Carter.

"If you complain one more time about the moving, the apartment, the fucking clothes," He shoves his hands through his hair. "Fuck, so help me God I'm going to kiss you until you shut up."

Kiss me?

The thought actually makes my heart beat faster while butterflies explode in my stomach.

It looks like he's counting to ten, then he says, "You start work tomorrow. Where the fuck would you have found the time to do all of this, or even find a place to stay? It's done. Say fucking thank you and let's get on with our lives."

He follows after Daniele and I hear him say goodbye to her. "Daddy has to go to the office but I'll be home for dinner, okay."

"Yes, Daddy," her sweet voice answers him.

He comes back out and pins me with a hard glare. "If you don't want to live with me, you are welcome to move, Della. Just know that my daughter will stay here."

I'm so angry I'm going to spit fire. He's been working on my nerves ever since I agreed to this mess.

"You're a control freak," I snap at him as he stalks to the door.

He glares at me before he leaves the apartment.

I tighten my ponytail as I look around me. A penthouse. This is no place to raise a child. Danny loves to run and climb. She's going to break something and Carter is going to have a heart attack.

I start to remove anything that can hurt Daniele and shove it as high as I can. I make sure all the doors and drawers are fitted with safety catches so Danny won't be able to open them without an adult nearby. I need a screwdriver. When I can't find one I take one of his expensive butter knives and start to install the safety door at the bottom of the stairs. I don't know what's up there and I don't care.

Hours later, I'm done making sure there's no way that Danny can get hurt. When I go check on her and Jamie, I find them both asleep on the double bed in Jamie's room.

This is the first time Jamie will have a room of her own. This is the first time Danny will have a room of her own. I need to do this for them.

I go to Danny's room and start to unpack all her clothes. Carter went crazy and practically bought our child every piece of clothing there is on the market. I look at all the stuffed animals and just shake my head. I understand that he's trying to make up for three years, but he can't keep doing this. I want Danny to appreciate everything in life and she won't learn to if he keeps giving her everything her little heart wants.

When I'm done with Danny's room I go check what the food situation looks like. I open the fridge and pinch the bridge of my nose when I see a six pack of beer, two bottles of water and an half full bottle of wine.

"Great, our first dinner will be alcohol."

The front door opens and Carter comes in. He places a bag on the counter before looking at me.

"Have you calmed down?"

I smile sweetly at him. "Welcome home, honey. Can I get you beer?" When he scowls at me I go on, "Or wait," I open the fridge and wave over the contents inside, "would you rather have some wine."

He shoves the bag towards me. "I got food. Stop with the bitching."

I look in the bag and see that it's fish and rice. I'm going to cry. No, first I'm going to lose my mind, then I'm going to kill him, and then I'll go to jail. Then I'll cry because I'm in jail for killing an asshole.

I rub both my hands over my face and calm down, reminding myself that this is all new to Carter.

"Daniele is allergic to fish. We need to sit down and go over everything she likes and don't like." I grab my bag and stalk to the door.

"Where are you going?"

"To the store so I can grab a few things that we will need."

166

I close the door behind me and walk towards the elevator. The doors open and as I step in and turn around, it's in time to see Carter walking toward me. I press the button to keep the doors from closing until he's inside.

We only make it two floors before he presses a button that stops the elevator.

"I'm sorry," he surprises me with an apology. "I'm new at this."

I let out a shaky breath and nod. "I know. This is a learning process for both of us."

"Let's go to the store together. I need to see what kind of food you get so I can make sure it's always in the cupboards."

"That's just it, Carter. You have to calm down with all the spending. You can't buy a year's supply of stuff for a three year old. She's a little person. She doesn't need a hundred dresses. She'll pick three and she'll wear them until they tear from all the use. You're wasting money."

He rubs over his jaw and it makes a rough sound from his day old beard. "Okay."

"I know this is new for you, but it's new for us too. I didn't grow up around money. Jamie and I have shared a room all our lives. Jamie wore my hand-me-downs. I wore second-hand clothes donated from the church."

When he grinds his teeth I quickly go on, "I'm not telling you this because I want to be pitied. It's always been my life. I had good days and bad days, just like you. I'm only telling you so you know how different our lives are. I start to panic when you throw money around as if it's nothing. I've learned to save, to use coupons, to be careful with money. You need to meet me in the middle."

"I didn't know," he whispers.

"You never asked."

He nods. "This goes both ways, Della. I've never lived with a woman. It's only been me and my dad. I'm going to do things wrong. I don't know any of the rules when it comes to living with a woman."

I shrug and smile at him. "I was ten when my dad died. Jamie can hardly remember him. We're pretty much in the same boat. We're going to do stuff that will upset you. We'll all just have to learn to get along."

"Can we start over?"

"Yeah, let's go get our daughter some food."

Chapter 26

CARTER

Shopping with Della is crazy on a whole new level. Every sweet I took, she just put back. She even spoke to me in her stern Mom voice. That's some serious scary shit.

When we get back home, Jamie is waiting for us with a jar in her arms. The words *swear jar* is written over the middle of it.

"Alright, kids." She holds the jar out to me. "You owe the jar thirty dollars for all the f-bombs and five dollars for the b-word."

"You're fucking kidding me," I say, not believing this shit.

"Make that an even forty-five. Another ten for the f-bomb."

Della starts to laugh but Jamie pins her with the same look that makes her quickly swallow the laughter

"Let me just place the bags on counter." While I pay my fine, Della unpacks the bags.

Daniele comes running from her room, yelling, "I'm made a poo-poo in the big toilet."

"Dammit, I forgot about her seat."

"That will be five dollars," Jamie says, taping the jar.

I try to open a cupboard but the thing is stuck. "What the hell?"

"That's another five dollars, and you have to remove the safety clip first."

I look at Jamie and take my wallet out again. I shove a hundred in the jar. "For the rest of the night. Now show me how to remove this thing."

Jamie unclips it quickly then hands it back to me. "Now you do it."

"Why?"

"So Danny won't open them and get hurt."

"Oh." After my fourth try I get it right. When I turn around Della is already busy preparing the Mac n Cheese.

"That's my favorite," Danny says as she's struggling to get onto one of the stools.

I go stand behind her and pick her up. Helping her to balance on the stool, I keep standing behind her so she doesn't fall backwards. She leans back against me and looks up at me with a huge smile. "Love you, Daddy."

Her words slam my breath from me.

I knew Dad loved me but he wasn't one to say it. I can't remember if I've ever heard those words in all my life. At least not directed at me.

I press a kiss to Daniele's head before I hand her to Jamie. I walk away before they can see what her words are doing to me. I'm just about to head up the stairs when I trip over something and slam the side of my head against the wall.

"Fuck it!"

Della is the first to come running. "What happened?"

I look down at the weird contraption that's blocking my way up the stairs.

"What's this? Have you turned the place into a death zone?"

"It's a safety door so Daniele doesn't go up the stairs." She looks at me, then darts forward. "You got hurt."

There's concern in her voice as she reaches up and presses her cool fingers against my forehead.

"Mommy, you have to make Daddy better," Daniele says, her little face tight with concern.

"Come," Della says as he takes my hand and pulls me to the bathroom. She wets a towel and presses it gently to my forehead.

When she's done, Daniele says, "Kiss it better, too."

Della's eyes dart from our daughter to me. She looks very nervous as she stands on her toes. She places her hands on my shoulders and pulls me a little forward. Her lips are soft as she presses a kiss to my forehead and I can't help but smile. She still smells like crushed apples.

When she's done kissing it all better there's a flush on her cheeks.

"Yeah, Mom. You have to kiss it better," I tease her.

She scowls up at me and the words just come. "Careful, babe. Looking at me like that will get you in trouble."

She starts to laugh, obviously remembering the first night we met. Her smile, her scent, her flushed cheeks – damn, it still has a way of screwing with me. She's still the only one I can see a future with.

Chapter 27

DELLA

I look at my reflection and sigh miserably. It's my first day at my dream job as cover designer, and I look like shit.

I'm wearing the best clothes I have, but the black pants are faded and the white blouse is stained yellow with time. I'm wearing my hair down for the first time in months. I've even curled it a little. It hangs well past my breasts. I pick up a strand and look that the split ends. I have to cut it this weekend. I've also put on a little eye-shadow with mascara. This is as good as it's going to get.

I walk out of my room and go kiss Daniele goodbye. At least we have time before Jamie starts school. I'll find a good daycare in the next few weeks.

When I walk into the kitchen, I'm surprised to see Carter still here. He looks devastatingly handsome dressed in a royal blue suit.

"Morning, Della," he says and his eyes sweep over me. "You look beautiful."

"Morning," I say, feeling very self-aware of the outfit. I hate that he's seeing me in these rags. After all, he is my boss.

"Hey, what's wrong?" he asks.

I force a smile to my lips. "I'm just nervous."

"Have some coffee before we go," he offers.

"We? You're taking me to work?"

That's bad. I don't want everyone thinking that I got the job because I know the boss. Even if it's true.

"We don't even work on the same floor, Della. No one will know about our relationship."

I spit the coffee out. "Relationship?" When I look down it feels like the ground is turning into quicksand. I've spilled on my blouse. Dammit!

"Yeah, we share a child," he snaps. "I'll wait while you go put on something else."

I grab some paper towels and start to dab at the coffee mark.

"Just go put on something else," he says again.

"I have nothing else," I snap as I toss the towel in the trash. "This is my best blouse."

"Let's go -"

"Don't even go there," I warn him as I position my hair over the stain.

He comes to stand in front of me and lifts my face so I'm forced to look at him.

"Why did you check on me last night when I walked into the safety gate at the bottom of the stairs?"

I shrug not sure where he's heading with this. I force the words out. "Cause I care," I huff.

The look on his face changes and it makes a nervous feeling explode in my stomach.

"I tried to see this for what it is, the mother of my child moving in so our daughter can have both her parents. I keep telling myself that you're just doing what's right for Daniele."

He frames my face with both his hands and our eyes lock. Tension starts to crackle between us and there's no denying that our attraction for each other is still very much alive.

Placing my hand over his, I lean my face into his right hand. He brings his other hand to my hip, pulling my body a little closer and it makes my heart beat wildly in my chest.

We just look at each other, while the attraction between us hangs in the air.

"I understand that you're cautious and used to doing your own thing," he whispers. "So much has changed and it will take time for the dust to settle. But, Della, I don't just want to take care of our daughter. I still want to try with you. I want to take care of you. And Jamie."

I hear his words and I'd love nothing more than an instant happily ever after, but that's not how life works.

"We can't just pick up where we left off, Carter. We were stupid. We got swept up in all the excitement of finally being finished with our studies. We have Daniele now. What if it doesn't work out between us? What do we do then?"

"That's a chance I'm willing to take," he says. "Look, I'm not saying we should jump into bed right away. We live together now. It's not like you can date. I can't bring someone over. We might as well try."

I pull away from him and frown. "I'm not going to be some consolation prize, Carter. If you want to screw someone then go ahead. All I ask is that you keep your women away from our daughter. As for me, I haven't dated in four years, and I'm not about to start."

I've forgotten how fast he moves. His hands are back on my face, keeping me from pulling away. The second I realize he's going to kiss me, it feels as if everything comes to a standstill.

His mouth crashes against mine and the intense wave of emotions that comes along with it, makes me lose my breath. His body pushes against mine until I bump into the counter. I grab hold of his sides as his tongue forcefully starts to dance with mine. He moves his hands to my backside, and picking me up, he sets me down on the counter. His strong body forces my legs open and he steps in between them. I feel his hardness straining through his pants and it makes my insides quiver with want.

He pulls away slightly and our racing breaths are all you can hear for a moment.

"I said I'd kiss you to shut you up. Next time I'm throwing you over my shoulder and carrying you upstairs."

I swallow hard and tell myself it's only lust that's making me like that idea.

He tucks my hair behind my ears and then frames my jaw.

"You can't tell me you didn't feel that. Let's try, Della. We deserve a chance. We can take it slow."

"Really slow," I whisper. I just hope I don't regret this.

Chapter 28

DELLA

Carter wanted to show me to where I will be working, but I quickly stopped him. I have to do this on my own. I don't want to be favored or hated because I know the boss.

When I step out on the twenty-fourth floor, there's no one at reception. I'm thirty minutes early because Carter has a meeting. Not that I mind. It gives me time to look around.

Looking at all the offices, I start to get excited. I wonder where my desk is. Will I get along with my co-workers?

"Hey gorgeous," a man says behind me.

I swing around and watch as a skinny middle-aged man with thinning brown hair and pale blue eyes walks toward me.

"I'm Stew Roberts. Are you new here?"

"Yes, it's my first day," I answer, hoping I don't sound too nervous. "It's a pleasure meeting you, Mr. Roberts."

We shake hands but when I start to pull back, he tightens his hold on my hand. I can't seem to keep eye contact with him, and it bothers me. I really want to make a good impression but instead an uneasy feeling skitters down my spine.

"The pleasure is all mine. Call me Stew. Welcome to the Indie Ink graphics team."

I swallow hard on the anxious feeling swarming in my stomach and nod. Finally, he lets go of my hand, and I resist the urge to wipe my hand on my pants.

I get a feeling I need to stay away from this guy.

"Do you have any idea where I'll be sitting?" I ask to speed things along.

A look of surprise washes over his face and then he smiles broadly.

"Yeah, of course. Follow me." I follow him down the hallway, right to the end. He points to a desk that's situated right outside an office. "You can sit here for now."

"The secretary is on vacation," he says. "Make yourself comfortable until they show you where to go and get you loaded on the system."

Disappointment washes over me. Carter said I would be working with the graphics team.

"How long is she on vacation for?"

"Two weeks. I don't know where Mr. West is, but I'm sure when he's back he'll get you all settled."

I force a smile to my face as I step around the desk. I tell myself it's just temporary. It will give me time to get used to everyone and to brush up on my graphic skills.

The morning is filled with a haze of faces and names as Stew introduces me to the team. He's constantly hanging around me and it's making me feel uneasy.

I'm sitting at the desk in reception, contemplating whether I should go up to Carter so he can give me some work. I hate not having something to do. It makes the day so much longer.

When I see Stew walking toward me, my stomach starts to burn with tension. This guy is just too much.

He walks around the desk and comes to stand behind me. When he leans over me, I freeze. This can't be professional. I might not have worked in an office environment before, but I'm not an idiot.

He places a pile of documents in front of me, and when he speaks, his stale coffee breath wafts over me. "I can see that you're bored. Let me show you where the copy room is, then you can make us some copies of these documents."

I lean to the side so that there's more space between us. Right now this asshole is making Carter look like a saint.

When he walks around the front of the desk, I let out the breath I've been holding. I rise to my feet and pick up the stack of documents.

We start to walk down the hallway when he asks, "Have you lived in New York all your life?"

"No," I answer not wanting to encourage him to ask personal questions.

"Where are you from?"

I suppress a sigh. "North Carolina."

When we get to the copy room, I'm disappointed to see that he's hanging around and not leaving me alone for a little while.

"You can go back up, I'll be okay," I try to encourage him to leave. Lord knows, I need some time to gather my scattered thoughts and emotions.

"Okay, just bring those to me when you're done."

Finally, I have some time to myself. I take my time making the copies, grateful that I have some work to keep me busy.

When I'm done I take it back up to Stew. I place it on his desk and I'm just about to turn around and leave, when he says, "Thanks that saves me a lot of time. Hey, we should celebrate your first day after work." He smiles, and an unnerving smile flits over his face, making the uneasy feeling take up permanent residence in my chest.

"I can't, "I apologize. "I have a three-year-old daughter waiting for me at home." I've never used Daniele as an excuse before, and it doesn't sit right with me that I'm placed in a position where I have to.

He stands up and shoves his hands in his pockets. It makes the material of his pants stretch over a bulge.

Oh, my God, I'm going to be sick. This man is disgusting.

I leave his office and walk back to the reception desk. This is not how I pictured my first day going.

Finally, it's time to go home, and I quickly straighten out the desk.

"Your first day wasn't that bad, right?" Stew says as he comes to stand in front of my desk and I realize he's waiting for me.

Somehow, I manage to smile. "It wasn't. Thank you for introducing me to everyone. I hope you have a good evening, Stew," I murmur.

"Let me walk you down."

Ugh, just what I need.

I'm thankful when we get to the elevators, and there are a group of people already waiting. At least I don't have to be alone with him anymore.

It's my first day and I'm already dreading tomorrow.

Chapter 29

CARTER

I don't usually leave the office before eight pm, but I can't wait to hear how Della's first day went.

I drove us to work this morning so I could leave the car here. I like to have at least one car here should I decide to go for drinks after work. I have Peter waiting out front with the town car. He moves to open the door when he sees me.

"We're waiting for someone," I say as I turn around and lean back against the car.

My eyes search every face, as people start to leave the fifty-floor building. Glass Towers is an impressive building. The first twenty floors are made up of rental space.

My eyes zoom in on Della the second she steps out of the elevators. Her face is unusually pale and the dark circles under her eyes make them look huge. She keeps fidgeting with her watch as she rushes towards the exit. A man falls into step beside her, and when they reach the exit, he places his hand on her lower back.

I straighten out and frown darkly as he keeps his hand on her back. The man smiles broadly as they walk out onto the pavement.

I take a step forward as Della looks up, and our eyes meet. The last time I saw that look on her face was the night those guys were chasing her down the street.

My eyes snap to the man but Della rushes forward and takes hold of my hand. "Don't," she whispers as she starts to pull me away.

"This is our car," I snap.

Peter quickly opens the door.

"Get in," I grind the words out, as the asshole finally notices me.

There's a look of dismay on his face so he obviously knows who I am.

"Please, Carter." Della doesn't let go of my hand but instead starts to pull me inside.

I'll find out who he is and deal with him tomorrow. I slide in after Della and only then do I feel how cold her hand is. I place her hand on my thigh and cover it with mine so it will get warm.

"Who is he?" I growl, still seething from seeing his hand on her back.

"He's just a co-worker. Please, Carter, I can handle him. I have to work with the man. Don't make things worse than they are."

I stare at her until she meets my eyes. "Who the fuck is he?" I grind out.

"Stew Roberts," she whispers and just saying his name makes a look of disgust wash over her face. "He showed me around and introduced me to everyone."

The name means nothing to me.

"Where was Jaxson?"

"Who?" she asks and it's clear she has no idea what I'm talking about.

"You work under Jaxson, Della. He's head of the graphic department. Where the fuck was Jaxson?"

"I didn't meet anyone named Jaxson. Stew did mention that the secretary is on vacation and that Mr. West had to be in a meeting."

I dig my phone out and call Jaxson.

"Where were you today?" I bark the second he answers.

"In the Bradbury meeting," he says.

"Fuck," I snap, closing my eyes for a moment. I need to calm down. I forgot about the meeting. It's a huge deal for us. We might be taking over Bradbury designs. I need that company so our graphic and printing departments will be able to handle the workflow when we expand internationally."

"I forgot. How did it go?"

"Things are on track. I'll meet you at the office tomorrow morning to go over everything with you."

"Great. Before you go, who is Steve-"

"Stew," she says next to me.

"Stew Rogers, who the fuck is he?"

"He's a designer. What's this about?"

"I'll talk to you tomorrow," I growl, cutting the call.

I take a few minutes to calm down.

When Peter parks the car outside a clothing store, Della tries to pull her hand out from under mine.

"What are we doing here? I thought we were going home."

Hearing her say the word home and knowing she's referring to my place makes a warm feeling expand in my chest.

"What happened today?" I ask.

"Nothing. I made some copies for Stew, but that was all." She looks upset and tired.

I frown at her. "What copies?"

"Some papers for Stew. I didn't have anything to do so he gave me some of his."

"You're not his fucking secretary," I snap. I'm going to kill that fucker.

"Carter, you're scaring me." Her beautiful features are drawn tight with tension.

"You were supposed to meet with Jaxson. Jaxson West oversees the graphics team. You met him in college. He's one of the twins. He helped fix your truck."

"Oh," she finally understands. She takes hold of my arm. "Carter, I don't want you to do anything. I don't want people thinking that I can't handle myself. Stew was just trying to be nice."

I turn more in the seat and brush some hair behind her ear. I really like it down. It brings out the blue of her eyes.

"Babe, I can't ignore this. Roberts had his hands on you. He fucked with the wrong female employee."

Shock ripples over her features. "Please let it go."

"No. You will only report to Jaxson. Jaxson is one of the directors. Do you really think I would have you making copies for some fucker?"

"What are you going to do?" she asks, her eyes wide on me.

"I'm going to fire his ass, and then I'm going to kick his ass."

She scoots closer to me and I can see I'm in for a fight. "You can't, Carter. What will my co-workers think of me if you fire someone because of me? He didn't really do anything wrong."

"I'm not going to ignore this."

She bites her bottom lip and it only makes her look fucking sexy.

"I'll make you a deal," she says, a hopeful look replacing the upset one. "I'll let you buy me some outfits for work, which I will pay back with my first paycheck, if you don't fire him. You can move him. You can give him a warning. I don't care, just don't fire him."

Fuck, she's clever. She needs the clothes but she's stubborn enough to wear the same outfit for the rest of the month just to have her way.

"Fine," I say, a smile forming on my lips. "I won't fire him, yet."

"Yet?" She raises an eyebrow at me.

"Don't push your luck. An asshole like him will make another mistake and I don't give second chances."

"Okay. So it's a deal." She actually holds her hand out to me and we shake on it before we get out of the car.

Chapter 30

DELLA

My hands caress the charcoal silk dress that falls just above my knees. I've never worn something so pretty. The black heels are luckily not too high, so it's not too hard to walk in them.

I wish I knew how to do my make-up. It's the only part of me that's still lacking a bit. That and the haircut I need to give myself this weekend. But other than that, I actually look ready for work.

I feel more confident than yesterday, even though I'm not sure what today will bring.

Walking into Daniele's room where the girls have been spending most of their time, I smile at the sight of them finger painting. Jamie seems to enjoy it just as much as Danny.

"I'm off to work. I won't be late tonight." I press a kiss to both Danny and Jamie's heads.

"You look so pretty, Della." Pride shines from my sister's eyes and it's times like this that she seems so much wiser than her mere fifteen years.

I give her a smile before walking to the kitchen. I'm just in time to see Carter slip on his jacket. The white shirt stretches tightly over his muscular chest and the sight makes my abdomen clench.

I have to admit that Carter has changed a lot over the past four years. It must be the responsibility of being a CEO. The younger version of him wouldn't have negotiated with me.

"Morning, babe." He's been calling me babe since last night.

He takes hold of my chin and presses a lingering kiss to my lips. When he pulls back I let out a breathy sigh.

"So much for taking it slow," I whisper.

He smirks at me and taking my hand we walk to the door. "By taking it slow I meant that I'll at least wait a few days before I fuck you, Della."

I gasp at his words as tingles race over my body. I should be upset with him but I can't because I'm even more attracted to this domineering alpha-man than I was back in college.

When we get to the car, the driver opens the door with a smile.

"Morning, Peter."

"Morning, Miss Truman."

Last night I told him to call me Della, but it doesn't look like it's going to happen.

Once we're seated, Carter takes my hand, and like yesterday, he places it on his powerful thigh. His thumb gently caresses my fingers as he sits deep in thought.

Before I can think of something to break the silence, he says, "It's Daniele's birthday next month. I actually missed four years of her life."

I can't even begin to imagine how he must feel and I have no words of comfort to offer. I really don't think there are any.

He smiles at me. It's not the reaction I expected. "I'm going to throw her a princess party."

"She doesn't have any friends here to invite. Maybe we should take her to the park, instead."

"I'm not celebrating my daughter's birthday in a park, Della. Besides, she has friends. I'll invite the guys over. She needs to get to know her uncles."

"At a princess party?"

"Yes, and they will fucking dress up for her."

"If you say so." I try to suppress the smile at the image of a bunch of men playing dress up.

Chapter 31

CARTER

As we step inside the elevator, Della starts to play with her watch. I pull her hand away and interlace our fingers.

When the doors open she tries to free her hand but I only hold it tighter.

"Are you ashamed of being seen with me?" I ask as we walk past the offices.

"Of course not!" she snaps. "You know I don't want the people thinking I got this job because I'm sleeping with you."

"Babe, if you were sleeping with me you wouldn't be a graphic designer." I grin seductively at her and it makes her face flush red. "You'd be head of the fucking department."

"Good to know I can still sleep my way to the top," she hisses.

As we round the corner, the asshole comes out of an office. When he sees me, he darts back inside the office.

I walk into Jaxson's office and close the door behind us.

Jaxson gets up from his chair and walks around the desk.

"When are you going to redecorate this place?" I snap.

"When I grow tits and a pussy," Jaxson snaps back before he turns his attention to Della. "Morning, Della. It's good to see you again."

He reaches for her and gives her a hug. She can only return it with one arm, seeing as I'm still holding her hand.

When he pulls back, he smiles down at her, "I'm really sorry I wasn't here yesterday."

"Morning, Jaxson. It really was nothing. Carter's blowing it out of proportion."

"The fucker had her make copies," I say to Jaxson, wanting to deal with this so I can get back to my own work.

"I know," Jaxson says. "He told me everything the second I got off the elevator." Jaxson looks to Della. "Stew says he was just trying to make you feel welcome."

"He's not the fucking welcoming committee," I bite out.

"I'm well aware of that," Jaxson says. "I watched the security footage for yesterday."

Della's hand tenses in mine. My eyes dart from her pale face back to Jaxson's. "What did you see?"

He looks to Della. "If you don't tell him, he'll just watch it."

My eyes burn a path from Jaxson to Della. "Tell me what?"

"It really was nothing. He was just a little too friendly."

My eyes flick back to Jaxson. "Show me."

"Can't we just fire him and get on with our day?" Jaxson asks but he's already walking to his desk.

I let go of Della's hand and follow him. "If it was up to me, I'd fire him. Della made me promise not to."

Jaxson looks between us and a huge smile crosses his face. The smile vanishes the second he presses play on his laptop.

He proceeds to forward through a few hours of footage before he presses play.

I watch the fucker get up from behind his desk. When he shoves his hands in his pockets, Jaxson pauses the screen.

"Fuck," I growl. The fucker actually had a hard on, and he was practically shoving it in her face. He's dead.

I turn around and stalk out of the office. When I slam his door open, he darts up from the chair. He's pale, and sweat is running down the sides of his face, even though the AC is set on cool.

"S-S-Sir," he starts to stammer.

"Carter." Della grabs my arm, and I glare down at her. "You promised."

Fuck.

Looking at her pleading face, I know there is no way I can go back on my word. I won't win her trust if I lose my temper now.

I don't even look in the direction of the fucker. I glare at Jaxson that's right behind us. "He packs all his shit now. I want this office cleaned out today. He can either report to Mr. Meyers, or he can hand in his resignation."

"You're demoting him to the mail room?" Jaxson asks.

"He either sorts mail or he leaves. He has a choice. He can be glad Della isn't filing a sexual harassment suit against him."

I stalk out the office and pull Della after me. "Which office is hers?"

"The empty one next to mine," Jaxson says and then he closes the door behind him so he can deal with the fucker.

I walk into Della's office and close the door behind us.

"I just need a second to calm down before I go upstairs," I grind out as I take a seat in front of her desk.

I watch her as she places her bag on the table. She opens the blinds and looks out the window. A smile forms around her lips as she takes in the view.

"I can ask Charlotte to come see you about anything else you might need for your office," I offer. I just want to make her comfortable now that the mess has been dealt with.

She shakes her head. "Thank you, but I want to decorate it. I've never had an office before. It will be fun."

Feeling a little more in control of my emotions, I get up. Della walks over to me and standing on her toes, she presses a soft kiss to my mouth.

"Thank you, Carter," she whispers.

"I made you a promise -"

"Not about him," she says. She drops her eyes to my chest and starts to straighten my tie. "Thank you for everything. You're going to be an amazing dad and … and friend."

I lean down so I can catch her eyes again. "Just a friend?"

A shy smile forms around her mouth and it makes me want to kiss her until her lips are swollen.

"Fine, I'll promote you to boyfriend status for now," she says, but quickly adds, "Just remember, I won't hesitate to demote you."

I press a kiss to her lips and smile. "I'll see you at five, babe."

Chapter 32

DELLA

I wake up with a smile. Today is Danny's birthday. It's also the first birthday where I don't have to work seeing as it's on a Saturday and I'm off on weekends.

I throw the blankets back and quickly get dressed in a pair of shorts and t-shirt. I run to Danny's room, excited to wake her up.

Carter is only accepting fifty dollars a month from me for the clothes we bought. I'll pay him fifty dollars for the rest of my life. At least it left me with plenty to buy Danny a pink princess outfit for today, and to save so I can take Jamie shopping before she goes back to school.

When I get to Danny's room, I find Carter leaning against the door where he's watching our sleeping daughter.

He's wearing a pair of jeans with a black t-shirt, but he's still as handsome as when he's dressed in one of his suits. I know I asked him to take it slow, but I didn't think he would take it this slow. It's been five weeks since we moved in and all he's done is hold my hand and kiss me.

"You wake her," I whisper.

He gives me a kiss on the forehead before he walks over to her bed.

"It's time for Daddy's princess to wake up," he whispers as he presses a kiss to her forehead.

Her tiny body stretches and her sleepy eyes open. She smiles at him. "It's my birthday."

He picks her up and kisses one of her chubby cheeks. "Yeah, you're a big girl now. Happy birthday, my princess."

"I'm four," Danny says, holding up three fingers.

He helps her hold up four, then presses a kiss to her tiny palm. "Daddy got you a present."

"Yay!" She bounces up and down in his arms.

I can already feel the prick of tears, but when he places her on the bed and kneels on the floor before her, emotion overwhelms me.

He takes something from his pocket and when he holds it up, I see that it's a chain with a heart locket. He opens it up. "It says *Daddy's Princess.*"

"I'm your princess," she yells excitedly.

"You're more than that." He clips the chain around her neck. "You're my world. There's nothing I won't do for you." He holds the tiny heart between his fingers. "This is my heart, Daniele, and it's all yours."

A tear sneaks down my cheek, and I quickly brush it away.

Daniele sees me and quickly climbs off the bed. "Look, Mommy. Daddy gave me his heart."

I crouch down. "I see. It's beautiful, baby. You need to look after it, okay. It's special."

"I'm not taking it off."

Her little face beams with happiness and I have Carter to thank for it.

Chapter 33

CARTER

When Rhett walks through the door I start to laugh until tears are running down my face.

He's dressed as a jester, bells and all.

"Someone needs to take a photo," I manage to get out between gasping for air.

"Yeah, I'm rocking this shit," he says.

"That will be five dollars," Jamie says as she goes to the counter to grab the swear jar.

I start to laugh again until I fall back on the couch. I'm going to die of laughing today.

"What the fuck is that," Rhett asks.

"That is another ten dollars," Jamie says with a huge smile.

I can't handle the laughing anymore.

"You're shitting me," Rhett says, but he starts to laugh as he takes out his wallet. He shoves a couple of hundreds in the jar. "That should cover me for the night."

Jamie just shakes her head and places the jar on the counter again.

She's dressed in a baby blue gown.

"You look really beautiful, Jamie," I say.

Her smile widens and she looks down at the dress. "You thinks so?"

"I know so."

"Did you get a shotgun?" Rhett asks as he sits down across from me.

"For what?"

"All the horny dicks that are going to be trying their luck with Jamie. Once you're done scaring them off you'll have to start all over again with Danny."

"Fuck, Rhett. My kid is four." I take my wallet out and hand Jamie the ten dollars. "I don't want to think about stuff like that."

When Marcus arrives, I'm surprised to see Leigh and Willow. I know that he and Willow has an on and off thing going. I wonder how Jaxson is going to feel when he sees Leigh here."

"Welcome to my princesses party," I say as I get up.

I kiss Leigh and Willow on the cheeks, then shake Marcus' hand.

"Does Jaxson know?"

Marcus shrugs. "Not my problem. It's time they sort out their shit anyway."

"And you thought my daughter's birthday party was a good place for that to happen?"

"Shit, sorry man. I'll phone Jaxson and give him a heads up."

"You do that, and you owe Jamie five dollars."

"Why?"

She comes to stand in front of him with the swear jar.

He just shakes his head and pays the fine.

"Daddy," Daniele yells as she comes running into the living room. She looks beautiful in her princess dress. I catch her and swing her into the air which makes her giggle out loud.

I point to Rhett. "Look, Uncle Rhett is a jester."

"What's that?"

"He's a clown, baby."

"Yay!" She claps her hands and I set her down so she can go climb all over Rhett.

Jaxson walks in and I start to laugh again. He looks like a knight, wearing armor and shit. The man can hardly walk straight.

"What were you thinking?" I laugh.

"Do you know how hard it is to drive with this on?"

I just shake my head.

"I can't even scratch my balls," he mumbles which has me laughing again.

When Logan comes in with Mia, my eyes instantly dart to Rhett. He gets up while still holding Danny and walks over to us. He presses a kiss to his sister's forehead and shakes Logan's hand.

I have to admit I'm a little surprised. I didn't think a day would come where he would give his blessing to any man.

A flash of pink catches my eye and my mouth drops open. Della looks breathtaking as she walks into the living room. I watch as she greets the guys. She looks happy seeing her old roommates.

"Where's Evie?" I hear her ask.

"I haven't heard from her in a while," Leigh answers.

My eyes dart back to Rhett and I don't miss the look of concern.

"When last did you talk to Evie?" I ask him.

He shakes his head and puts a wiggling Danny down so she can run around.

"It's been almost four months. Her phone has been disconnected. I'm going to need some time off so can go look for her."

"Sure. Whatever you need."

Chapter 34

DELLA

We both stand for a while, watching our little girl sleep.

The party was a huge success. She had so much fun. The guys went out of their way to make her feel special.

Carter takes my hand and pulls me from the room. I'm surprised when he leads me to my room. He closes the door behind us and locks it which makes my stomach flutter with nerves.

"I've been thinking," he whispers. He places a kiss to my forehead and I close my eyes, just breathing him in.

"Yeah? What have you been thinking?"

His eyes caress my face in a way that makes my heart expand.

"We should go look for a house. I want a garden Danny can play in. "

I smile at him, liking that idea very much. "She would love that."

"Four years ago you gave birth to our daughter," he whispers while looking at me such wonder it makes me feel emotional. "The first time I saw you, you took my breath away. I knew you were strong but I had no idea just how strong. All I know of my mother is that she walked away from me."

I place my hand against his cheek wishing I could erase that memory from him.

He kisses my palm and takes a chain from his pocket. My mouth drops open at the sight of the broken heart hanging from it.

My eyes dart up to his and when I see all the emotion on his face it makes tears well in my eyes.

"I swore I would never trust a woman after my mother broke my heart." I can't keep the tears from rolling over my cheeks and I don't even bother whipping them again. "I'm giving you my broken heart, Della. I can only trust you with it."

I wait for him to clip it around my neck before I throw my arms around him. I press a kiss to his lips and whisper, "I'll keep it safe. I promise."

He crushes my mouth under his and the kiss quickly turns heated.

He reaches behind him, and breaks the kiss long enough to pull his shirt over his head. I catch sight of his muscled chest and I struggle to keep my mouth from dropping open.

He's always been the most beautiful man I've ever seen, but now he's pure perfection. He's all hard muscle, not an ounce of fat on him. I have a sudden urge to lick his golden skin.

"Carter, you're..." I whisper, unable to tear my eyes from his perfect chest.

He leans down, and, placing a hand on either side of my head, he kisses me, a warm and tender kiss that turns my bones to rubber.

He reaches behind me and unzips the dress. It falls to the floor, pooling around my feet.

This moment is perfect. We can finally be together with nothing between us.

My eyes dart up to his and I feel the spark of heat between us.

I feel a little self-conscious about standing in front of him in only my bra and panties. Just like any other woman that's given birth, I have stretch marks. I definitely don't have the same body I did when he last saw me naked.

My first instinct is to cover myself, but the scorching look in his eyes makes me stand still.

"You're even more beautiful than I remember." There's so much lust in his voice, it settles like a bolt of fire between my legs.

Heat spreads through my body and tiny tongues of desire lick at my skin.

He quickly strips out of the rest of his clothes. I take in his naked perfection, so exquisitely male in every way.

I reach behind me and unhook my bra, never taking my eyes from his. I let the material fall to the floor and immediately Carter's eyes drop down to my breasts. He makes a sound of pure pleasure which gives me the guts to step out of my panties.

"Fuck, babe. The sight of you leaves me breathless."

I can't remember a time when I wanted something as much as I want his hands on me right this second.

Carter is mine.

I'm his.

Shivers rush over my skin at the thought that we're finally together.

He reaches for my face and brushes his fingers down my cheek.

I let my eyes drink in his features, his dark lashes and those deep brown eyes that never miss a thing. My eyes keep trailing down his face to his straight nose and then they land on his full lips.

I lift my hand to his face and brush the tips of my fingers over his skin, just enjoying the feel of him.

I stand on my toes at the same moment that he leans down, and our mouths find each other's. At first, the kiss is slow, but then our tongues meet, and I can't help but moan in delight.

Carter thrusts his tongue deeper and he takes a step closer, crushing our bodies together.

Sparks shoot through me and go straight to my abdomen. Damn, he tastes so good. How have I lived without him the past four years?

He makes me burn up until all that remains of me are smoldering ashes. I press my breasts harder against his chest wanting to feel more of him. I feel his erection pressing into my lower belly and the thought of him being so close to me is a heady one.

He devours me with wild and hungry kisses until our breaths are racing into each other.

I love the look on his face. It's one of pure adoration and lust. I could get addicted to it.

Chapter 35

CARTER

I pull her right against me and soak in the pure pleasure of feeling her naked body pressing against mine before I push her back to where the bed is.

I follow her onto the bed kissing her hungrily, like the starving man I am. I want to lose myself in her. I kiss her with every ounce of love I have in my heart.

Finally, Della's naked under me again. It's nothing short of a miracle that's kept me from fucking her sooner. I first needed to win her trust before taking our relationship to the next level. It's been the longest month of my life.

I pull slightly away from her and look down at her lust filled eyes. I need to drink in every inch of her.

My heart feels light for the first time. I feel relieved and at peace. I have my daughter and the woman I love. Damn, I'm a lucky man.

Right now, I just want to lose myself in Della. Her long, silky brown hair is spread over the cover. Her cheeks are flushed with desire.

Once again, a fierce protectiveness fills my chest to the point where it feels like I might explode. We belong together. I knew it the first time I laid eyes on her. She was mine that day. She'll be mine for all eternity.

I close the distance between us and trail gentle kisses over her skin.

"Carter," she sighs blissfully.

Fuck, I can listen to her saying my name all night long. She makes it sound like a prayer.

I'm so hard for her. My cock throbs against her stomach. Once I'm inside of her, it will only take a matter of seconds for me. It's been too long.

I'll make it up to her right through the night, but right now I have no control. I can't hold myself back anymore.

I close my mouth over her breast and groan at the taste of her skin. She still tastes like crushed apples. I take my time licking and sucking until she starts to roll her hips against me.

I brush my hand over her toned stomach and then over her pussy. She's so fucking wet.

"You're so ready, babe," I groan against her silky skin.

"Please, Carter. I need you now. Please."

What my woman wants, my woman gets.

I quickly get off the bed and grab a condom from my pocket. I roll it on before I crawl back onto the bed.

She opens her legs wider to accommodate my shoulders. I press a kiss to her pussy before I start to devour it.

I alternate between licking her clit roughly and desperately sucking at her pussy. Her arousal is addictive making me lose all control.

When her body starts to tense, I know she'll be coming soon.

"You taste so fucking sweet," I growl against her pussy and it makes her moan.

I push two fingers inside her so I can feel when her orgasm hits.

"Carter," she breathlessly moans, lost in ecstasy and rubbing her pussy all over my face.

When her inner walls starts to greedily suck at my fingers I pull away and crawl over her body. I line my cock up with her and surge into her tight, wet heat with one powerful thrust.

"Fuck … fuck, it's heaven," I growl at the perfect feel of her around my cock.

Her muscles ripple and her muscles grip me tightly, making my hips surge forward.

Our mouths meet in a frenzy, and I start to drive my cock into her, thrusting and grinding until moan after moan escapes her.

Every nerve-ending is on fire as I watch her orgasm beneath me.

"Carter," she breathes, and the pure pleasure in that one word sends me over the edge.

A tingling starts in my abdomen, making me move faster. Just as the world explodes around me and my cock starts to jerk inside of Della, she cries my name. She spasms around my cock, milking every last drop from me.

I can't bring myself to move yet. I remain still for a few seconds, just absorbing the feel of Della.

When strength returns to my body, I push my upper body up and look down into her eyes, filled with love and satisfaction.

I place a quick kiss to her lips. "I'll be right back."

As I get rid of the condom, I remember the last time we were together. I quickly finish up and sigh with relief when I walk into the room and she's still lying on the bed.

We crawl under the covers and I pull her naked body into mine. I stare at her beautiful face until her eyes fall shut as she drifts off to sleep.

I pull the cover away from her body and look at every mark that was left by the pregnancy. This woman carried my child and the proof will forever be marked on her skin. I smile at the thought that I've branded her in a way that no other man can. Della is mine.

Chapter 36

DELLA

As I wake up, I snuggle into the warmth enfolding me. Only my eyes are visible from beneath the blankets that smell like Carter. I smile as a sigh of happiness escapes my lips.

I take a few minutes, just staring at his peaceful face.

He asked me to move into his room. Last night I gave in and we spent the night carrying all my stuff up.

I slip out of bed, getting clean clothes from the dresser before I walk into the bathroom. I place the clothes on the counter, and reaching into the shower, I open the faucets.

The shower is twice the size of the one downstairs. I'm so going to enjoy this.

I'm just about to step under the water when Carter comes up behind me. He wraps his arms around me and pulls me back against his chest.

He nuzzles my neck and then whispers. "I could get used to seeing you naked every morning."

"That can be arranged," I say, turning in his arms.

"You know there's no way you can get rid of me now."

I let my hands slide over his muscled chest, loving the feel of him. The memory of his ass flexing in my hands as he was thrusting inside me last night instantly turns me on.

I smile up at him. "You might want to rethink that. I might just tie you to the bed so I can have my wicked way with you all the time."

I don't know where the bravery is coming from to say these words to him. Maybe it's because his eyes are filled with love for me.

"Don't make a promise you can't keep," he says all seductive.

He leans into me, placing a tender kiss on my lips. It feels so good to be desired by this man.

"You make me feel like a woman, something precious," I whisper against his lips.

"You're not just a woman, Della. You're a fucking goddess and you should be fucked like one," he growls, lust swirling in his eyes.

He crushes his mouth to mine in a hungry kiss that makes my insides clench with desire. If I had panties on they would be soaked right now.

I love everything about Carter. I love the way he kisses me, the way his hands caress my body, the way he makes love to me. I'll never get my fill of him.

I let one hand travel down his body until I find his cock, hard and ready. Wrapping my fingers around him, I squeeze hard before I start to stroke him.

Carter lets out a moan and starts to thrust into my hand.

Glancing up at him, all I see is desire, his lips slightly parted.

He pushes me back until we're both in the shower, then he circles his hips against my hand.

"Feel that? That's me wanting you right now. Hard and fucking fast," he says, his voice deep and strained. It sends shivers racing over my body from pure delight of being able to do this to him.

He takes hold of my hips and turns me around so that my back is to him

"Put your hands against the wall and bend over," he growls.

Dammit, I love when he goes all dominant male on me.

I place my hands against the wall and lean forward so that my ass is on full display for him. His hand caresses a hot path over my back and swell of my ass. He brings his arm around the front of me. His forearm comes up between my breasts and his fingers close around my throat.

His other hand slips between my legs from behind. I let my head fall back against his shoulder and take hold of his wrist, just holding onto him. His fingers brush over my clit and it instantly draws a moan from me.

"I want to hear you say it, babe. Say you're mine," he demands.

He pushes one finger into me.

I push my ass back against him and when I feel his rock hard cock, I start to move up and down, rubbing myself against him.

"I'm yours," I whisper breathlessly into the water.

He pushes another finger inside me and then starts to rub my pussy while he thrusts hard against my ass.

This is so erotic, feeling his hard cock sliding against my ass while his fingers work magic on my clit. I let go of his wrist and cupping my breasts, I squeeze them hard. It draws a low groan from Carter which only makes me braver.

"Fuck yes," he growls, moving even faster until I'm caught up in a cloud of pleasure.

I slip one hand down my front and cup my pussy. I slip a finger inside myself along with his and we move together as wave after wave of pleasure crashes over me.

Suddenly, he pulls away from me. He spins me around, grabs hold of my ass and lifts me up. I wrap my legs around him just as he slams into me. Feeling his huge cock spearing me draws a cry from me. The orgasm hits hard and it makes my body quiver.

Carter fucks me hard until I feel raw and swollen. He takes all of my weight as he finds his own orgasm. I feel his body jerk against mine until the last of the pleasure flows through him.

I wrap my arms around his neck thinking we can definitely start our days like this from now on.

Chapter 37

CARTER

My life has changed so much over the past few months. I can't believe it's been just three months since I walked into that diner.

I found a good school for Jamie. I've just finished printing all the forms so Della can complete them and get everything ready. We can drive to the school tomorrow and enroll Jamie.

I pick up the phone on my desk and dial Della's extension.

"Della Truman," she answers.

"We need to change your last name," I say.

She's quiet for a few seconds and I start to worry that I've pushed too hard.

"Carter Hayes, you better not be proposing to me over a damn phone," she snaps.

It instantly brings a smile to my face. "Fuck, I wouldn't dare. You'd cut my balls off and I'd like to have more children."

"Is there a reason for this call?" she asks.

"Yeah, get your ass up to my office. I found the perfect school for Jamie."

She squeals and then the line gets cut. I lean back in the chair and watch the door. Minutes later my door bursts open and Della comes running in. She slams it shut behind her, then starts to clap her hands as she runs to me.

"Show me. Show me Show me!"

I start to laugh at her excitement.

"It's a good school. I think she'll fit in there. They have a lot of activities she can choose from."

When we're done looking at all the paperwork, she throws her arms around my neck and kisses me hard.

When she pulls back I drink in the sight of her face shining with happiness. I brush the back of my knuckles over her cheek, down her neck, and over her nipple. My eyes drop to her cleavage. I love this dress on her.

"You know I love this dress."

She grins up at me. "I know."

I kneel before her and shove the silky material up her legs. "Hold that."

She quickly grabs the material, bunching it in her hands.

"Carter," she whispers. "What if someone walks in?"

"Babe, you're the only one who dares to just come in. The rest know not to even try."

She still looks worried as she bites her bottom lip.

I grin wickedly up at her. "Babe, relax."

"Relax," she mumbles as I drag her panties down her legs.

I let her step out of them and shove them in my pocket.

I cup her pussy and place a kiss to her thigh. Then I open her up and start to devour her.

"Dammit, Carter," she breathes. "You're a dream come true."

I force her legs to open wider and thrust my tongue inside of her. I lap at her sweet arousal as my cock strains against my pants.

I pull away from her grab her hand and lead her over to the massive window.

"Hands on the window and bend over."

She quickly does as I say. I lift the material over her ass, then unzip my pants. I pull my aching cock free and position it at her entrance. When I thrust into her, she slams into the window with a whimper.

I grab hold of her hips and start to ruthlessly pound into her. I'll never get enough of fucking her.

My body tenses over her as she starts whimper my name. I keep thrusting as I come inside of her. Her orgasm hits hard and for the first time a cry tears from her. I quickly cover her mouth with my hand as I continue to fuck her until her body slumps against the window.

"Wow," she breathes as I pull out.

My come trickles down her thighs and it's only then I realize I didn't use a condom. I pick her up and carry her to the bathroom that's situated in my office. I wet some towels and gently clean her. Seeing how swollen she is and knowing it's because of my cock being inside her, makes me want to fuck her all over again.

"I forgot to use a condom," I state the obvious.

I toss the towels in the trash and look at her. There's a smile playing around her lips.

"As long as you fuck me like that, I'll let it go."

232

"You're a fucking tease," I growl.

She holds her hand out to me. "My panties, Mr. Hayes."

I shake my head. "I'm keeping them, Miss Truman. Consider it punishment for seducing the boss in his office."

She looks a little unsure. "Are you serious?"

"Yeah," I say, grinning.

"You want me to walk around the office without panties on?"

"Yeah."

She nods and biting her bottom lip she places a hand on my jaw. She presses a kiss to my lips, then whispers, "Fine. I'll walk around your office without any panties on. Later on, I might be sitting at my desk remember how hard you were fucking me against the window." She bites my bottom lip. "My hand might slip under the table and find its way to my bare pussy and I'll just have to finger-fuck myself."

I'm fucking hard as steel for her.

She starts to walk away, and as I reach for her she darts forward, laughing out loud.

"I'll see you later, Mr. Hayes."

"Fucking tease," I growl as I watch her swing her ass all the way out of my office.

I pull my zip up and try to position my cock in a way that will be less visible, just as my office door opens again. Della walks back in and her eyes instantly go to my hand on my cock.

"Don't let me stop you. I forgot the forms."

She grabs them from my table and walks out again.

"Yeah, I got myself a cock teaser."

Chapter 38

DELLA

Making sure I have all the papers that I'll need for Jamie, I go down to the copy room. Most of the staff is on lunch, but I chose to stay in the office so I could get everything ready for tomorrow's visit to the school.

Someone closes the door of the copy room, and I look over my shoulder. I watch as Stew saunters closer to me.

Damn, why couldn't he be on lunch, as well? I haven't spoken to him since my first day.

"Afternoon," I say, looking back to the copy I'm making of Jamie's last report card. She's going to be so excited when she hears about the school.

Suddenly, Stew grabs hold of my hair and yanks me backwards. The shock of the attack draws a cry from me. For a moment, I'm too stunned to realize what's happening.

I manage to rip myself free from him, but I lose hair in the process which makes my scalp sting something fiercely.

When I swing around and I see the mean look on his face, my body starts to shake as adrenaline starts to pump through my veins. Quickly, I dart to the side, putting some distance between us.

This man is crazy! I have to get away from him.

A million horrible scenarios start to race through my mind, as I watch him glare at me with hatred. It makes an icy grip of panic tighten its hold on my insides.

I glance at the closed door, and knowing that I have to make a run for it, I dart forward.

Stew moves fast and comes right at me. He looks like psycho that's about to rip my heart out. As he reaches for me, I scream and duck to the side, but he grabs hold of my arm, yanking me backwards.

Stew's voice is a vicious growl that agitates every nerve ending in my body, and leaves my insides quaking. "It's because of you! It's your fault that I got demoted. It's your fault that I was forced to take a pay cut."

I lose my balance but it doesn't stop him from dragging me away from the door. My knees shaft against the carpet and I try to rip free from his hold.

"Let me go," I shriek as panic starts to override my common sense. I try to pull my body away from his, but he's stronger than me.

"Don't do this, Stew. I can talk to Carter. I can make him listen."

I'll tell him any lie to make him calm down.

My movements grow frantic with panic and the air grows hot and stuffy in the room.

Oh my God! I don't want to die in a copy room.

Stew lets go of my arm but before I can get up, he takes hold of my feet and drags me forward. The movement makes my dress bunch up around my thighs and cold horror washes over me. I'm not wearing any panties. If the dress goes any higher, this madman will see that I'm bare.

I stop fighting and grab at my dress, forcing the material down. While he drags me over to the far corner I do everything I can to keep the material in place.

I start to panic as a suffocating feeling of fear weighs heavily down on my chest.

"Let me go," I spit the words at him.

When I see the crazy look in his eyes, I know for certain that he's planning on killing me. I let go of the dress and start to kick at him with every bit of strength I have in my legs.

My heel slams into his neck and he falls back on his ass, gasping for air.

I quickly turn my body around and crawl away from him. I don't get far before he grabs hold of my foot, yanking me back to where he wants me.

He crawls over my back and wraps his disgusting fingers around my neck. He starts to slam my face against the carpet and I try to turn my head so it won't hurt as much.

"You," he growls. "Because of you, I lost it all!"

His fingers tighten around my throat until his nails dig into my skin. I start to gag for air, and when I don't manage to take a breath, I go insane with fear.

"I'm going to kill you so he knows what it feels like to lose everything," Stew hisses.

This can't be my end.

I want to see my daughter grow up. I want to see Carter walk her down the aisle. I want to hold her babies in my arms. I want to grow old with Carter.

My vision starts to blur and my body spasms. I hear a crashing sound and then voices are yelling.

Stew's weight is lifted off me, and then more hands grab at me.

I yank and hit, but it feels like I'm moving in slow motion. All I hear is the ragged sound of my lungs gasping for air.

I keep hitting, kicking and growling like a possessed person while I crawl away from Stew. Dread has taken over every part of me. In this terror induced state, there's only one thought - I have to survive for Daniele. I have to survive this somehow.

Nausea overwhelms me and I start to vomit. I try to keep moving, but my strength is fading fast.

Oh, God! I need to survive for my daughter.

Someone grabs me from behind and I try to swing my elbow into them. The movement throws me off balance and I fall to the side, as my body starts to convulse and another wave of nausea overwhelms me. The person pulls my body against theirs and pulls my hair away from my face.

My throat is on fire when I finally stop vomiting. "Stop. Just stop," I cry.

"Della," someone cries through the haziness of hysteria that's enveloping me.

When the person doesn't let go of me I start to scream until my throat feels like it's raw and bleeding.

"Get him out of here," the person holding me shouts. "Get him the fuck out of here before I kill him."

Through blurring tears I see people move around me. Someone kneels in front of me and for a moment I don't recognize him.

"Della, you're going to be okay. The paramedics are on the way," he says.

I try to suck in some air but the pain is too much. A wail tears through my ravaged throat and I slump forward.

The man frames my face with his hands, and his touch is cool on my overheated skin. He lifts my face to his and it's only then that I recognize him.

"Logan?" I rasp.

"Yeah, Sweetheart. Try to stay still for us. Rhett's holding you. You're safe."

"Rhett?"

"I've got you, babe," I hear him say from behind me. His voice is thick with tears. Every bit of strength I have vanishes and my body sinks against his.

Chapter 39

CARTER

My phone rings but I ignore it. I need to finish signing these documents so Charlotte can have them back before I leave for my two pm meeting.

Finally, the thing stops ringing.

I get another three documents signed before my office door burst open. Charlotte's pale face has me up on my feet in a second.

"What's wrong? Are you feeling sick?" I rush to her just in case she faints.

She grabs my arm and starts to pull me from the office. "You need to go. They're in the copy room. Someone attacked Della."

Shaking my head, I frown at Charlotte. "What?"

Then the words sink in. *Della has been attacked.*

I run from my office and when I reach the elevators, I repeatedly slam the button until the fucking thing opens.

I step inside and impatiently wait for the doors to close. When they finally shut in front of me, I slam my fist into the mirror. A crack splinters through the mirror and I quickly step back as it crashes to the ground.

I open and close my fists as fear overwhelms me.

Della.

My Della.

My mind races, not really focusing on anything of substance.

The elevator doors open, and as I step out shock shudders through me. The building security is all over the place. I watch as paramedics run towards me. The run by me and into the copy room, and it's only then that life returns to my body.

I follow the paramedics, and when I step inside the room my world starts to spin. Della is on the floor and Rhett is holding her. Logan is on his knees in front of her and he starts to move so the paramedics can get to her.

My eyes dart around the room and if feels as if someone is throwing punches at me. I see the vomit. Fuck, the stench hangs sour in the air.

I look back to Della as a paramedic reaches for her neck. She starts to struggle in Rhett's hold, raw wails tearing from her.

I start to walk towards her. It feels as if something else has taken over my body. I want to run to her side, but for some fucked-up reason, I can't.

Logan places his hand against my chest. I see his mouth move but nothing he says makes sense. I can only hear Della.

Rage engulfs me, and I walk right by Logan. One of the paramedics tries to stop me, but I shove him out of my way.

I reach for Della as she looks up and the fear on her face fucking destroys me. I sink to my knees next to the woman I love more than life itself. My heart is thundering in my chest as Rhett let's go of her. Her body shoots forward and I catch her as she slams into me.

Her breaths sound like painful gasps that are grating her throat raw. I wish I could breathe for her.

"Babe," I say, but it doesn't sound like my voice.

244

She tries to pull herself up against me but there's no strength in her body.

Abruptly, the reality slams into me and it feels as if I'm thrown into a nightmare.

I wrap my arms around her and hold her shaking body to me.

"What the fuck happened?" I growl at Rhett.

"Someone attacked her. We were in the printing room when we heard her screaming," Rhett says. I've never seen him so pale and upset before. "The fucker was on top of her, strangling her."

"Who?" I hiss.

Rhett shakes his head. "I don't know. The guards dragged him away."

"Sir, we need to get her to a hospital," the paramedic says, drawing my attention back to him.

Fuck, he's right.

I start to pull back, but Della just moves with me.

"Babe, let them look at you," I whisper.

She shakes her head, burrowing deeper against me.

The paramedic reaches for her arm, but Della starts to panic. "No.No.No.No.No." She practically crawls through my arms to get behind me, and it makes me lose my mind.

"Don't you fucking touch her!"

"Carter, they have to check her," Rhett says, half positioning his body between me and the paramedic.

What he says makes sense, but I can't let anyone near her. I gather her in my arms and pick her up. She buries her face in my neck and her body shudders in my arms.

I shake my head at Rhett. "I can't let her go. She will never forgive me if I let her go. You go -" Tears overwhelm me and I swallow hard to try and control them. "You go get a doctor. I don't care what you have to pay. Get a doctor and bring them to the apartment. I'm taking her home."

"Fuck, Carter," Rhett hisses. "You can't just take her. She needs to give a statement. This is a fucking crime scene."

I glare at him as I hold her tighter. "You will have to pry her from my dead fucking body. I'm taking her home. The cops can take her statement there. A doctor can look at her there."

"You can't -"

"I can and I fucking will."

I walk out to the room, not paying attention to anyone. When I exit the building, I'm relieved to see

Peter already waiting with the car. He's supposed to take me to the two pm meeting.

I slide into the backseat and cradle Della on my lap. I press kisses to her tangled hair. She's fucking cold. I sit forward and without moving her from my lap, I struggle out of my jacket.

I wrap it around her before holding her tightly. She's stopped crying but the blank look on her face really worries me.

My phone starts to ring and I quickly fish it from my pocket.

"What?" I hiss, barely in control of my emotions.

"The paramedics are following you. Please don't give them shit. Let them look at her while I get a doctor."

"Fine."

"Danny," Della croaks.

"What's that, babe?"

"Danny. Don't let her see me."

"Fuck." I forgot. I quickly phone Jamie. When she answers the phone I can hear Danny laughing. "Jamie, take Danny to the park. Buy her an ice cream and let her play there for a little while."

"Why?"

I take a deep breath so I don't lose my temper. "Please, kiddo. Take Danny to the park."

"Okay. I'll take her for an hour."

"Thanks."

When we get to the apartment, I'm careful not to jar her body as I carry her to the apartment. I take her upstairs so Danny won't see her by accident. I've just placed her on the bed when there's a knock at the door. I quickly cover her with a blanket, then run to open the door.

I'm relieved when Logan comes in with the paramedics.

"Will you stay down here for in case Jamie and Danny come back from the park? Call me so I can talk to Jamie."

"Sure." He gives me an encouraging smile.

I quickly race back up the stairs with the paramedics behind me. I walk around the bed and sit behind Della.

"Babe, they need to look at you. I'm right here. Let them fix you up."

I haven't even had a good look at her face. When the paramedic starts to work on her, my eyes are drawn to every bruise. The marks around her neck are the worst. They're purple and on places her skin is broken.

I don't know how much time passes before a doctor arrives. The paramedics leave the room, allowing the doctor to take over.

People start to come and go. Everyone asks questions which Della answers as if she's on automatic pilot. I guess she is, considering everything that's happened.

I find out from the police that it was Stew Roberts. It was revenge for what I did to him.

I should have killed him when I had the chance.

Chapter 40

DELLA

It's been a week since the attack. I'm just waiting for the bruises to fade so I can go back to work.

The first three days I couldn't keep in any food. All I remember was feeling sick to my stomach. The rest is all a blur.

Carter stayed with me for four days before I told him to go back to work. The sooner things return to normal the sooner I'll be able to move on.

Stew has been charged with aggravated assault. Once he's been sentenced I'll never have to see him again.

I look at my reflection in the mirror and brush the tips of my fingers over the marks on my neck.

I almost died.

Another human being almost took my life.

I'll never forget the crazed look in his eyes. I'll never forget the promise of death in his voice. I believed him.

Surprisingly, I have no nightmares when I sleep. The real nightmare is when I'm awake – the memories. I know it will take time to deal with what happened.

The men have been in and out, constantly checking on me. I owe Rhett and Logan my life.

I'm sitting in a chair, staring out the window when Marcus comes into the room. I'm surprised to see him here. He never comes to visit unless Carter is here.

He comes to stand next to me and leans against the wall, just staring out the window. When he doesn't say anything, I go back to staring out the window myself.

"I know we're not as close as you are with the others, but I wanted to tell you that I do care."

I try to force a smile to my lips, but it's too hard.

Marcus crouches next to the chair and his blue eyes catch mine. I've never actually looked at him. His eyes are a little darker than mine.

"I know what it feels like, thinking you're going to die. I know the fear you felt. I know the thoughts you were thinking."

Tears start to well in my eyes.

"For days, it's all you smell. You can't eat because it's all you taste. When you close your eyes it's all you see. I fucking get it, Della."

A tear rolls over my cheek and as I look away from him, he reaches for my chin, turning my face back so I'll look at him.

"It gets better." I've heard those words before, but it's the first time I believe them. "Not today. Not tomorrow. Not anytime soon. But it does start to fade until you can manage it."

"How?" I breathe the word through my tears.

"I can't tell you how. It's different for every survivor."

The word survivor makes me reach for his hand. He tightens his fingers around mine, and for a while, we sit together.

"I'm a survivor," I whisper.

Marcus stands up and gives my hand a tight squeeze. "You're a survivor, Della."

He presses a kiss to my forehead before he starts to walk away.

"Marcus," I call out to him.

"Yeah," he says from over his shoulder.

"You should come visit more."

A smile pulls at the corner of his mouth. "Sure."

Chapter 41

CARTER

Della started working last week. She's only been going in half days. At least I got her to compromise on that. If it were up to her she would've worked full days.

Next week Jamie starts school. Della couldn't go with me to enroll Jamie because the marks were still too visible.

I sit and watch as Della and Jamie look at a shirt for school. Danny's sitting at my feet, and playing with a doll.

Jamie grabs a dress and holds it up against her body. She starts to walk funny, and when she swings around, she squints her eyes and pushes her front teeth over her bottom lip. I chuckle at the funny face she's pulling.

"I'm gonna be the prettiest gal at the ball," she says in squeaky voice.

Danny starts to laugh next to me and then Della laughs.

Emotion wells up in at the sight of her smiling face. Fuck, I missed hearing her laugh.

Later when the girls are both asleep, I sit on the bed looking over some documents for the takeover we're busy with.

The bathroom door opens and when Della comes out naked, the papers fall from my hands.

She crawls onto the bed and over my legs. She keeps her eyes on mine while she shoves the papers onto the floor.

She unzips my pants and I let her pull it off. I yank my shirt over my head and lean back again. She places a kiss to my thigh, then her fingers wrap around my cock. She strokes me lightly and it sends tingles of pleasure racing over my skin. A moan bubbles up from the back of my throat as she starts to stroke me faster.

I'll do anything she wants, and it's not because she's literally got me by the balls, but because I love her with every ounce of my being.

She leans a bit forward and my eyes widen. Fuck, she's going to take me in her mouth. The thought alone makes my cock jump with anticipation in her hand. My breath hitches and my stomach tightens.

She pumps my cock once more time before her lips wrap around me. A breath of hot air bursts over my sensitive skin, again making my cock jerk.

She starts to suck while twirling her tongue around the sensitive head of my cock, almost making me come right then.

"Fuck, Della. It feels fucking good. Don't stop," I growl as my hips start to thrust, wanting to plunge my cock deeper inside her mouth.

She pulls back and licks me from base to tip, instantly making pre-cum form on the tip.

I'm not going to last long. Fuck.

She slides her mouth fully over me again and then starts to bob her head up and down, sucking me hard.

I lean my head back and watch her suck me. I reach for her and let my hands tangle with her silky hair. Feeling her head move beneath my hands while watching her lips glide over me as she sucks me hard, fuck, it's the most erotic thing I've ever seen.

My breaths come faster over my parted lips and my insides clench with pleasure.

She moans and I feel the vibration all the way to my balls, and it sends me over the edge. My ass muscles tighten and I lift off the bed in a hard thrust.

"Fuck, I'm going to come, babe," I groan as my hips start to thrust hard and fast, searching for that explosion of ecstasy in my gut.

She tightens her fist around the base of my cock, sucking hard one more time. It's all I need to make the orgasm shudder through me, hot and fucking intense.

After the last of the pleasure ebbs away, I sink back on the bed, totally drained.

"That was fucking perfect."

She smiles proudly at me. "I was aiming for perfect, Mr. Hayes."

She climbs on my lap and presses a kiss to my lips.

"Watching you come because I'm sucking you is such a turn on." Her tone is seductive and her eyes burn with lust.

I can feel her body trembling with need. She wants me just as badly as I want her. She wants me to fuck her raw. I'm going to torture her sweet pussy until she's aching for my cock.

When she tries to position herself over my still recovering cock, I stop her by taking hold of her hips. I just need a few minutes to recover and I'll be back in the game.

I see the question in her eyes until my fingers brush over her clit. I pinch her gently and her mouth drops open on a moan. Her nipples harden even more and I lean forward, taking one between my teeth. I bite down gently and a tremble rocks her body.

When I push a finger inside of her, I can feel how wet she is for me and it helps get me harder so much faster.

I pull my finger out and then, taking hold of my cock, I start to rub her clit until her hips rub shamelessly against me, her pussy begging for more.

Her cheeks flush with pleasure as she moans again. I drink in her soft features, her lips parting on her moans, her nipples hard as fuck, and her hips thrusting down on me.

Fuck, she's my life.

I'm going to fuck her and I'm going to enjoy every minute.

"Carter," she groans.

I keep teasing her pussy as I rub my cock over her opening.

"Say it, babe," I growl, wanting to hear the words from her panting lips.

"Fuck me," she moans her desire-filled eyes begging me.

I position the head of my cock at her opening and before I can thrust up she pushes down on me. The pleasure is overwhelming as she wildly starts to ride me.

I let my head fall back as the woman of my dreams fuck me raw.

The sound of our skin slapping, our breaths rushing, and our hearts beating off the charts, make this moment all the more perfect.

Her fingers dig into my shoulders and she starts to chant, "Carter … fuck …Carter," as a look of pure ecstasy washes over her face.

She moves faster as she chases her orgasm, pushing me over the edge. I thrust up hard as a shout escapes my lips. It's toe-curling, body-numbing, earth-fucking-shattering carnality.

She slumps against me and neither of us moves for a long time.

Chapter 42

DELLA

It helps knowing people with a lot of money. I didn't have to wait months before I got to testify against Stew Roberts.

He was sentenced today and I got to see how he was taken away in cuffs. It's was a liberating moment which I needed it.

The guys wanted to throw a party to celebrate but I stopped them. I'd rather have a quiet dinner with all my friends seeing as it will be Jamie's first day at school tomorrow.

She convinced me to use the money in the swear jar so we could take-out for everyone.

"Pizza," Rhett hollers as he sees all the boxes on the counter. "A meal fit for a king."

"My daddy's a king," Danny says as she goes to hug Rhett. "Are you a king, Uncle Rhett?"

He kisses her chubby cheek as he picks her up. "Not yet, baby-girl. I need a princess of my own before I can be a king."

"What are you then?" she asks innocently.

"I'm a legend, baby-girl."

He sets her down and she comes running over to me. "Mommy, he's a lege … a lege … he's my uncle Ledge."

I laugh and look over to Rhett. "Hey, Uncle Ledge." I wiggle my eyebrows at him.

"I like that. *Ledge.* Damn, I always wanted a cool name."

"Uncle Ledge, I want some pizza. Some of the cheesy ones." Danny starts to climb up his leg so he has no choice but to pick her up again.

I sit down at the kitchen counter as everyone starts to arrive.

Rhett starts to feed Danny, but she has to kiss his cheek every time she wants a bite. She's got him eating out of her tiny hand.

Chapter 43

CARTER

I wait in the kitchen for the girls to finish up. My apartment is filled with the smells of their different perfumes.

I glance around and smile when I see Danny's coloring book and crayons lying on the floor. Jamie's jacket lies over the back of one of the couches. Della's bag is on the counter. Everywhere I look, I see something that belongs to them. They've made this place their home. For the first time, I have a home with a heartbeat.

The girls walk into the kitchen and I place their lunch bags in front of them. I made one for Danny, too, even though she'll be getting breakfast and lunch at the daycare she's going to.

"It's a big day for my girls."

"You made us lunch," Jamie says, pulling a scared face. "Is it edible?"

"Ha-ha. Aren't you a funny one?" I smile when she looks inside the bag and smiles.

"I can get used to this." Jamie turns to Della and Danny. "Will you give us a minute? We'll be right down."

"Sure," Della winks at me and grabs all their stuff.

Jamie waits for them to leave before she turns back to me. I'm surprised when her chin starts to tremble and tears well in her eyes.

"I know you're only my brother-in-law, well almost. You just have to get the guts and ask her already." She wipes a tear away and looks down at her feet.

Emotion wells in my chest, realizing that she just gave me her blessing.

Then she looks back up and a tear trails down her cheek. I reach for her face and wipe it away.

"You're not just a good dad for Danny." She sucks in a breath of air and blurts the words out. "You're the closest thing I've had to a dad and I just want to say thank you. I love you, Carter."

Fuck. Tears start to fall as I hug her to me. She's the first one of the girls to say those words to me.

"I love you too, Jamie. You know I'll do anything for you, right?"

She pulls back and presses a kiss to my cheek. "I know."

"Good. Let's get you to school. I have a few boys to intimidate."

"What?"

I walk out of the apartment with Jamie right behind me.

"You're not going to embarrass me, are you?" she asks as we walk to the elevator.

"I wouldn't dream of it," I say with a huge smile on my face and I feeling ten-fucking-feet tall.

As the doors close I say, "I can't vouch for the guys, though. They're waiting down stairs."

She slumps back against the elevator and sighs, "In that case, I'm going to die of embarrassment."

Chapter 44

DELLA

"Just stop so I can run in," Jamie says as she looks nervously out the back of the car.

The guys are all following behind our car in a convoy. I've seen the secret smiles Jamie has been trying to hide. She's loving the attention.

As soon as Carter brings the car to a stop, he locks the doors.

"No!" Jamie starts to laugh as she tries to open the door. "I thought you loved me, Carter?"

"I do, that's why I'm doing this," he says with a huge smile. "You'll love me even more when all those horny dicks stay away from you."

"You owe the jar five dollars." She presses a kiss to Carter's cheek and then one to mine.

"I love you guys, now open the door."

My mouth drops open at their words of love. I've never heard Jamie say those words.

Carter unlocks the doors as the guys form a line outside Jamie's door. She gets out and starts to blush when Rhett turns his cheek so she can kiss him.

She has to kiss each one of them before they let her walk away.

I notice how all the girls are gaping at the guys and all the boys are staring at the cars.

I get a feeling Jamie is going to be very popular.

We all drive to the daycare and Danny starts to bounce in her chair. "It's my turn!" she shrieks with excitement.

I get out and unbuckle Danny from her seat. She jumps into my arms and presses a wet kiss to my lips. "I love you, Mommy."

I hardly have time to soak in the warmth of the words before she starts to wiggle in my arms.

"I love you, Danny," I say as I start to laugh.

"I know. Put me down now," she demands.

I laugh as I put her down and she runs around the car.

The guys are all crouching down so they're eye level with her.

She starts to press wet kisses to their cheeks.

"Love you, Uncle Marcus. Love you, Uncle Jax. Love you, Uncle Logie. Love you, Uncle Ledge." She shoves her fists into her sides and takes a huge breath. "It's hard work loving all of you."

I'm crying and laughing at the same time.

Carter picks her up and we walk her inside. She presses a kiss to his cheek and whispers, "I love you, Daddy."

He tightens his hold on our daughter, presses a kiss to her chubby cheek and whispers, "I love you most, Daddy's Princess."

∞∞∞∞∞

I'm woken by his arm slipping around me. He drags me over to his side of the bed, pressing my back to his chest. He buries his face in my hair and I hear him breathing me in.

"You still smell like crushed apples," he whispers. "You complete me, Della. Without you and the girls, my life would have no meaning."

His words make a lump form in my throat, which I try to swallow down.

"I like you a lot, Della Truman," he says.

"I like you too," I whisper.

His lips move down the side of my face and when he reaches my jaw, he says, "I love you, Della Hayes."

I turn my face slightly, until I feel his breath on the corner of my mouth and time freezes.

"You're the mother of my child, my lover, my best friend, but I desperately want you to be my wife."

I smile at him through tears. "You're the father of both my children." He frowns lightly. "Our four-year-old daughter and our unborn baby that's currently ten weeks old."

He moves fast, his mouth crushing mine. We both gasp at the impact, and then he kisses me hard. There's a hungry desperation to his movements. His tongue plunges into my mouth. It feels as if he's going to devour me.

I try to bring my hand to his face, but he grabs hold of my wrist and pins my hand to the pillow. He positions his body over mine I quickly open my legs to accommodate his size.

He's controlling and intense, and it robs me of all common sense.

He shoves the covers away and they fall to the floor. He yanks my panties down my legs and when he comes back up his mouth latches onto my pussy and he starts to devour me until I'm a thrashing mess, begging for release.

Everything about him is primal.

He shoves two fingers inside of me and I grab at his hair as he continues to suck and lick at me. Lifting my hips, I push myself closer to him, not able to stop myself from grinding against him.

I want to feel his hands on me as he fucks me rough.

He yanks his fingers out of me, and I feel as he shoves his pants down.

He makes me feel priceless, and in his world where he can buy anything his heart desires, that's saying a lot.

His hand covers my right breast and he squeezes hard until his fingers bite into my flesh. The mixture of pain and pleasure makes me clench with need.

He shoves his pants further down his powerful thighs. My eyes land on his cock. It's huge and thick, and I can't wait to have him inside me.

His fingers bite into the sides of my thighs and he pulls my legs open. I drink in the sight of him, as he pushes inside of me.

He slips his hands under my ass, and he pulls my cheeks apart, opening me as wide as I can go. He draws out of me, and the skin stretches tight over his cock.

I watch as he drives into me, stretching my opening until I'm swept up on high of shameless desire. I grab hold of the headboard as he starts to move faster and harder.

His hips surge violently, his pelvis crashing into mine. My body jerks with each hard thrust as he buries himself in me. He grinds his pelvis against my sensitive clit, tearing a helpless whimper from me.

I feel every inch of him, merciless and forceful as he strokes my inner walls until I'm whimpering for my orgasm.

I try to raise my ass from the bed, wanting to provoke him into fucking me senseless. Instead, he presses his body down on mine, pinning me to the bed with his muscular body.

"Della," he breathes my name, making it sound like a prayer. "Marry me."

He pulls out and slowly enters me. He's going to drive me insane.

"Yes," I groan, just wanting him to finish me off.

He keeps a torturously slow pace and it's starting to drive me wild. I dig my nails into his ass, and I try to urge him on by pushing him down on me.

He starts to move faster, the sound of slapping skin and sex filling the room.

"Yes," I gasp as my orgasm starts to build.

He slides in deep, making sure I take every inch of him. With each deep thrust, my body starts to wind tighter and tighter until it feels like I'm going to shatter.

Carter presses his forehead to mine. I feel his hard body against mine. His cock assaults me until I'm raw and it feels as if my heart is pulsating between my legs.

I feel his breath on my lips and it all works together, taking me so fucking high.

My body arches against Carter's as I whimper, "Yes."

My body starts to shudder under his and when he tenses over me, we come together. I wrap my legs behind his ass as he hammers into me, finally fucking me, as our bodies greedily ride out the pleasure between us.

He doesn't pull out, but instead, he holds me tenderly. We keep breathing each other's air as our eyes are locked on each other.

"I take that as a yes?" he says, smiling as he presses a kiss to my lips.

"I love you," I whisper against his lips.

THE END

Enemies to Lovers Series

Heartless, Novel #1 ~ Carter Hayes & Della Truman

Reckless, Novel #2 ~ Logan West & Mia Daniels

Careless, Novel #3 ~ Jaxson West & Leigh Baxter

Ruthless, Novel #4 ~ Marcus Reed & Willow Brooks

Shameless, Novel #5 ~ Rhett Daniels & Evie Cole

About The Author

Michelle Horst has changed to Michelle Heard.

Michelle is a Bestselling Romance Author who loves creating stories her readers can get lost in. She loves an alpha hero who is not afraid to fight for his woman.

Want to be up to date with what's happening in Michelle's world? Sign up to receive the latest news on her alpha hero releases, sales, and great giveaways → **http://eepurl.com/cUXM_P**

If you enjoyed this book, or any book, please consider leaving a review. It's appreciated by authors.

Acknowledgments

Sheldon, you hold my heart in your hands. Thank you for being the best son a mother can ask for.

To my beta readers, Morgan, Kelly, Kristine, Laura, and Leeann - thank you for being the godparents of my paper-baby.

A special thank you to every blogger and reader that took the time to take part in the cover reveal and release day.

Love ya all tons ;)

Made in the USA
Columbia, SC
04 October 2020